Charred Remains

Evan Bond

Published by Evan Bond, 2022.

This is a work of fiction. Similarities to real people, places, or events are entirely coincidental.

CHARRED REMAINS

First edition. May 16, 2022.

Written by Evan Bond.

Also by Evan Bond

Ethan McCormick Series
To the Wolves
Sins of the Mother

The After Death Series
After Death

Standalone
Death Can Wait
Getaway
Echoes of the Past
Charred Remains

Watch for more at https://www.evanbondauthor.com/.

For you... Yes, you!

Introduction

The campfire crackles and pops as the flames lick at the logs in the center of the circle. Two dark silhouettes crowd around the dancing flames, absorbing the warmth. The flickering light bounces over their darkened bodies. They are thin and frail. It seems they haven't eaten anything in some time. Their eyes seem locked on the campfire like they are waiting for a meal to spring forth and greet them.

My stomach rumbles and I realize I'm hungry too. It's been ages since my last meal. Or, at least, I think it has. I can't quite remember. For that matter, I don't remember where I am or how I got here. But those are questions best left answered another time. For now, I have the need to cozy up to the flames for its warmth. These frail beings must be doing it for a reason. Maybe I should follow their lead.

As I scoot in close to the flames, neither being moves. Even up close, I cannot make out any features. They seem like shadows over people. Being that they're the only people I've seen in a while, I shrug my shoulders.

Tree sap pops from inside one of the logs. It causes me to jump but the others do not stir. I assume they are already used to the sounds of the campfire. But another thought crosses my mind. What if they are deaf? It would explain why they didn't react when I approached.

"Excuse me," I say, my voice cracking. "Can you tell me where we are?" Neither of the figures moves. It confirms my suspicions.

Upon closer inspection, I can see the figures nodding along to something unheard. It's almost as if they are listening to someone talk. They move in unison. The movements are subtle. The longer I stare, the more I notice them. They can hear something I can't. I try to shut out all the noise around me and hear whatever it is they are listening to. I shut my eyes tight and focus on nothing. The sound of the wind through the trees, the soft coos of the owls, screeches of the bats, and the crackling flames all disappear. There is nothing now. Only silence.

Then the silence shatters. A voice whispers in my head. It's too soft to hear. I try harder to listen, but it's still too quiet. My eyes slide open and I look at the shadows before me, still huddling over the fire. I am doing everything they are doing. I don't understand why I can't hear these voices. Not one to give up, I try again.

My eyes shut, the noises fall away, and I feel a sense of vertigo inside my body. Like the ripcord was pulled on an invisible parachute. Now there is something more than a whisper. I can hear the voice! A deep growl of a voice in my head. Not quite human, but unlike anything I've ever heard before. I don't bother with trying to figure out who or what is talking. Instead, I listen to the words the voice has to say.

"Listen," it whispers. "And you will be set free."

I have no idea what it means. And yet, I feel like I might. Wherever I am, this is how I leave with this unseen specter whispering stories in my head. It is the only way to leave this place. There is nothing left to do but sit back...and listen.

The Ashes

The Stranger

He was tired of the dingy motels. The rotten smell of must and social decay stung his nostrils. There was no sadder place for someone like him. Russel always thought of himself as talented. His writings were that of a genius. He often thought of himself as the reincarnation of Edgar Allan Poe. The stories he wrote were masterpieces and the world would see that one day.

For now, the world only saw the struggling artist. Poor economic filth that plagued the city. He moved from motel to motel and paid his way with what little he scraped up by taking temporary jobs. It wasn't much, but it allowed him to focus on his true passion. Writing.

Russel did not care about having a stable income. He had stories to write. Novels to craft. A full-time job would only get in the way of his masterpieces. Besides, who needed some thick-headed boss breathing down his neck when he was his own boss? Nobody told Russel what to do. There was no giving that up.

The blinking cursor stared him in the face as if to mock him. For the past few days, Russel could not get a single word on the page. It was terrible writer's block. No word was good enough. He deleted everything he typed before a sentence could form.

It was beyond frustrating. It was far past infuriating. This was his story to end all stories. This would be the masterpiece to rocket his name to superstardom. He would be the biggest name in horror to have ever lived. He could feel it. If he could only get this last story finished.

But the words weren't there. No matter how hard he tried to get past the writer's block, it held strong. He hoped he could chisel away at it if he forced the words. There was no getting past it. Russel would give anything to overcome this writer's block. This was his *Mona Lisa*. His *Tell-tale Heart*. People would remember his name after this story. He felt it.

He closed his eyes and pictured his dream life. No more seedy motels. No more squalor. He would live the high life. The fancy house, the beautiful women, the fast cars. It would be his for the taking. Russel imagined the movie deals. His works would grace the big screen and become the biggest sensation since *Harry Potter* or *Game of Thrones*. Russel would hardly be able to go out in public without people recognizing his face. He imagined book signings in great venues and the biggest bookstores around the world.

A knock at the door broke Russel from his daydream. He craned his neck and stared at it thinking he must have misheard. There could be no one at the door for him. Who would be here to visit him? The knock came again. This time, he knew it was real.

Russel stood from the desk and approached the peephole. Outside stood a tall man in a nice black suit. The stranger pulled back his left sleeve and glanced at a watch like he was late for an important meeting. Russel could only guess he was the motel manager, though the fancy clothes were a bit much for some dump like this.

He pulled open the door and stuck his face into the humid air. The stranger stood there with a warm smile. He looked trustworthy enough. Russel didn't see the harm in talking to the man.

"Can I help you?" He asked, trying to sound as pleasant as possible.

"So sorry to disturb you," the stranger said with a nod. "I couldn't help but notice you may be having a bit of trouble with your manuscript and thought I may be of service."

A flash of cold froze through Russel's body. How could this stranger know that? Were there cameras in the room? Was he being watched? If so, why? This man couldn't know what he was doing in this motel room.

"I'm sorry. I don't mean to frighten you. I can tell by your pale face I already have," the man chuckled. "Let's just say I can make all of your dreams come true."

"What, like a genie?"

The stranger laughed again.

"Of course not! There's no such thing as genies. What I am is far more complex than that. I think you people would label me a devil, which is terribly offensive."

He laughed again.

"I think you'd better leave, sir," Russel warned.

"If you wish. But you'll never finish that manuscript. You'll stare at that blinking little cursor for several more weeks before you take your own life. And that would be a shame for someone with your talent. I think the world could use your stories. But if you would prefer me to leave-"

"No, wait," Russel interrupted. "Please come in."

He pulled the door open and let the stranger inside. Russel shut the door behind him and turned to face his new visitor. He looked harmless enough. Calling himself a devil had Russel on edge. The things he claimed to know were impossible. There had to be some truth to his story. He was willing to hear him out for a chance at the life he always wanted.

"I don't have a lot of time, Russel, so I'll cut to the chase. I can give you everything you've ever wanted if you only shake my hand. The fame, the fortune, the book deals. It can all be yours with just a simple shake."

"And what do you get out of it?" Russel asked.

"My boy, I'm a devil, as you people call me, what do you think I want in return?"

"My soul?"

The stranger laughed.

"Maybe in the old days when a soul meant something. These days, well, never mind. No, all we take is a share in your success. That's all."

"Really? The devil wants money?"

"A devil, not *the* devil. And I still don't like the description. Just a share in that success. That's all we take."

Russel thought it over in his head. This all seemed crazy. It couldn't be for real. But what did he have to lose? It would be no different from having an agent. A share in his money is all it took to be famous and successful. He had to try.

"Fine," Russel said. "Deal." He proffered his hand to the stranger.

"So much quicker than I expected, Russel. A wise choice."

He gripped Russel's hand and held it tight. Russel watched as the stranger's features began to morph until he was staring into his own eyes. The stranger had become an identical twin. It was like looking into a mirror. Before he could ask questions, a pain in his chest erupted and he dropped to his knees. He looked up at his own face staring down at him.

"I told you, Russel," the stranger said. "A share in the success. Your books will be world-famous. And I will be the face of your career." The stranger let out a laugh as Russel's world grew dark.

Oak Trees

The night was coming to an end. Only embers remained of the logs Craig had once put on the fire. They radiated orange and yellow light in a small ring around the firepit. Craig swirled them around in a whirlwind of ash and glowing sparks. A small fire burst from the coals for a few seconds before snuffing out completely. Now, there was only darkness.

It was time for bed. Craig had a busy morning ahead of him. He would need to break down his camp before continuing on the trail. Another twelve hours of hiking lay before him. Then he would make another campsite and another fire. This was his first backpacking excursion. All other hiking trips had been day trips. He had booked all other camping trips ahead of time. This was all new and exhilarating.

Craig unzipped the small one-man tent and crawled inside. He lay in his sleeping bag, listening to the relaxing sounds of nature around him. The soft hoot of an owl echoed in the distance. Cicadas buzzed like waterfalls high above in the treetops. Nocturnal animals scurried about the forest floor, scavenging for food. It was all like white noise for Craig. He fell fast asleep.

Somewhere in the early hours of the morning, something jolted Craig from his slumber. Before he could question what had pulled him from sleep, his bladder began to ache. He yawned as he crawled towards the opening of the tent. In the silence of the night, the zipper seemed to echo through the trees. If any animals were sleeping nearby, they were sure to wake up.

Walking a few feet from camp, Craig relieved himself behind a tree. The morning air was dewy with a slight chill. He shivered. When he finally finished, Craig retreated towards the tent. A branch broke in the distance, catching his attention. He stared through the sheets of darkness, trying to see what had caused the sound. He was not afraid. Craig knew it was more likely to be a racoon or armadillo. His knowledge of nocturnal life was limited, but he knew enough to get by.

Seeing nothing, Craig unzipped his tent once again. As he did, a loud thud broke through the night air like a large tree branch had fallen to the ground. Now he wondered if a bear lurked nearby and had pushed over a rotten tree. Fishing into his tent, Craig pulled out his flashlight. He focused the beam around the campsite and saw nothing but trees.

With a shrug, Craig crawled back into his tent and zipped it shut. As he settled back in for sleep, another loud thud echoed in the forest. Only this time, it was closer. Craig grew worried now. If it was a large animal such as a bear, it could pose a real threat. Not something he wanted to come face to face with while in the woods.

Once again, Craig unzipped his tent and peered outside. Clicking on the flashlight revealed nothing near camp. An endless sea of tree trunks. As he clicked off the flashlight with a shrug, something moved in the distance. Without hesitation, he clicked the flashlight back on. There was nothing there.

In the beam, he saw only the large tree trunk of a magnificent oak. The trunk was thick and round and yet seemed to be swaying from side to side in an unnatural way. Craig could only see the base of the trunk in the cone of his flashlight. He panned the flashlight up towards the top of the tree and stopped. There were no branches or leaves. The top half of the tree seemed to be missing. In its place was a strange, round object. It took Craig almost a minute to realize what he was looking at.

The pale, round figure on top of the tree trunk began to move. It craned left and right like a person cracking their neck. A thin line spread out from one side to the other and began to open into a wide smile. The thing standing before Craig sent a shiver down his spine. A tall figure with a large, round head. Its sawdust-colored head sat atop a body made of tree bark. Razor-sharp teeth lined its gaping maw. Craig could see no eyes on the creature.

He did not wait for the monster to move. Instead, Craig leaped from the tent and ran down the trail. After a few seconds of running, he heard loud thundering booms coming from behind. They came to an abrupt halt. He dared a look over his shoulder and saw something that turned his blood cold. The giant tree-like monster had bent over his camp and devoured the tent whole. Craig ran until his lungs burned and then ran some more. His only hope was to leave the forest behind and never return.

Reflection

She would be leaving for her date soon and she still had not picked out what she was going to wear. Elizabeth stood in front of the mirror, holding up dress after dress. She tossed the unworthy ones into a pile over shoulder. None of them had given her the look she was going for.

It had been a while since she had dated, so she was ready to go all in. But she didn't want to look desperate. She didn't want to look like a slut or a prude, either. Riding that line was harder than she expected.

Elizabeth pulled a skirt out of her closet and held it up. The fabric almost reached down to her mid-thigh. She laughed and tossed the skirt into the pile. The skirt was one of her favorites, but she feared it would send the wrong message. This guy would think he was getting lucky at the end of the night. Then again, he might be. She hadn't decided yet.

Standing before the mirror in nothing but her underwear, Elizabeth looked at herself. Her mind was laser-focused on her looks, more so than ever. She was never one to obsess over her appearance, but tonight would be a different story. She needed to be at her best to lure this guy back to her bedroom. If that was what she wanted.

"This better go well. I seriously need to get laid," she said to her reflection. She gave herself a disapproving look through the mirror. "Hey, don't look at me like that. Girls got needs, too."

She gave herself a coy smile but almost fainted when she didn't see the same smile come back through the glass. Instead, her reflection had frowned.

"What the fuck?" she said, stepping back. It had to be a trick of the light or something. There was no way her reflection had done something different. That was impossible.

Elizabeth leaned closer and peered into her own eyes. Her heart fluttered faster as she expected to see the orbs dart in a different direction from her own. But her reflection held firm.

"All right, maybe I'm more nervous for this date than I thought." She smiled and reached back into her closet for the next dress.

Returning her gaze to the mirror, she stopped short. The dress slipped from her hand, dropping to the floor. Her heart slammed against her ribcage; her breath sucked from her lungs. Fear gripped her harder than she had ever felt before. Elizabeth stared at the empty mirror before her. Her reflection had vanished.

"What the fuck? What the fuck? What the fuck?" she stammered, sliding her fingers through her hair.

This wasn't real. This couldn't be happening. She was having a stress-related hallucination of some kind. It had to be. The date was weighing heavier on her mind than she thought. Elizabeth shut her eyes and shook her head, hoping to clear it.

Elizabeth fought with herself to open her eyes. She feared what she would see when they opened. When they finally did, she saw her reflection staring back at her. A cool sense of relief washed over her. It had been all in her head. At least, that was what she thought until she looked closer at the reflection. It no longer wore the same clothes. Instead, it sported the mini skirt Elizabeth had held up earlier and a skintight tube top.

Reflection Elizabeth ran her hands up and down her own body. Elizabeth found herself frozen in fear. Things like this didn't happen. They couldn't happen. Only in horror movies. Not real life. She had gone crazy. It was the only explanation.

The reflection continued to run its fingers across her body as it swayed its hips back and forth. Elizabeth still could not get her legs to move. They felt glued to the floor. As the reflection ripped open the tube top revealing her breasts, it flicked its tongue like a snake. Elizabeth let out a blood-curdling scream and found the strength to move. She grabbed a shoe from the closet and threw it straight into the mirror, hoping it would break.

Except, the mirror did not break. Instead, the reflection caught the shoe. Her hand had shot out of the mirror and snatched the shoe out of the air, pulling it back into its world. Elizabeth took a step backward, finally finding the strength to move.

The reflection laughed as it began to lick the shoe up and down with an elongated tongue. Elizabeth felt like vomiting as she watched this mutated version of herself. She did everything she could to hold it down for fear of taking her eyes off the reflection. Elizabeth wanted to run out of her room, but that would mean turning her back to the mirror. The thought of it filled her with more dread than she imagined possible.

The monster pressed her breasts against the inside of the mirror and laughed. "A girl's got needs," it said in a perfect imitation of Elizabeth. Hearing the doppelganger speak sent a chill down her spine. Then the reflection did something Elizabeth had not expected. It reached to the side and pulled another figure into frame. Another copy of Elizabeth. Only this one was not a copy. This was her true reflection.

Elizabeth felt her hair get yanked up into the air to match her reflection. Her feet began to lift off the ground, though nothing was holding her up. Somehow, the doppelganger was able to interact with Elizabeth using her reflection. Elizabeth screamed and kicked through the air, trying to get free. She watched in horror as the doppelganger version of herself slid its tongue all over her body. Elizabeth could feel the moisture from the disgusting thing.

The tongue snaked its way around her body before forcing itself down Elizabeth's throat. She gagged and choked, trying to get the taste of the slimy tongue out of her mouth. Nothing physical had entered it, but she could see it happening in the mirror. A bizarre and disconnected sensation fell over her that overloaded her senses.

Finally, the doppelganger pulled back its tongue and dropped Elizabeth to the floor. Her head smacked the tile and the world went dark.

When her eyes opened again, the world was fuzzy. It took several minutes for her vision to clear. Elizabeth sat up and found herself face to face with her mirror. She almost leaped to her feet and ran until she realized it was only her reflection now. The doppelganger was gone.

Elizabeth spotted a lump on her forehead from where she had hit the floor. She reached up and touched it, wincing at the pain. To her comfort, the reflection reacted just as she had. It was her reflection once again. For some reason, the doppelganger in her mirror had left her alone.

She let out a sigh of relief, hoping the nightmare was over. Elizabeth turned around to leave her bedroom, wanting to get as far from her room as possible. When she turned to face the bedroom door, she realized it was no longer where it should have been. Instead of being off to her right, it was now on the left. Everything in her room had flipped.

The blood in her veins turned to ice as she slowly turned back to face the mirror. The twisted reflection of herself had returned. It smiled and gave her a wink. It reached over to pick up the cell phone on the nightstand. Elizabeth found herself doing the same. She could only watch helplessly at her own movements as her thumbs typed a message to her date.

Be there soon.

With that, the doppelganger turned to leave the bedroom. Elizabeth mimicked her every move without being able to stop. She could only see the world around her in brief flashes of reflections from the corner of her eyes. Every so often, the doppelganger would turn and give Elizabeth a playful wink.

Lucky Number Thirteen

There she was. As beautiful as he remembered. The sparkle of the black paint had faded over the decades, but he recognized his girl anywhere. He remembered cruising around behind the wheel, windows down, music blasting. It reminded him of his younger years. The youth he so desperately wanted to relive. Damn getting older.

"She needs a bit of work," the man holding the keys said. "But these classic cars were built to last. You can get her fixed up in no time."

"As long as this baby purrs, I'm ready to take her off your hands." Clyde rubbed his together, awaiting the feel of the steering wheel in his grip.

"Man, this is a 1960 GTO. She doesn't purr. She roars." The two men shared a laugh. "Here," the man said, tossing the keys. "Start her up and see for yourself."

Clyde held the keys for a moment. This was it. He was going to hear her come to life. A sound he hadn't heard in ages. He wondered what it would be like. Would the memories all flood back at the same time? Would nostalgia wash over him like a flood? Clyde was nervous but excited about it all.

He climbed behind the wheel and ran his hands across the dashboard. "Hey Dahlia," He said with a smile. "Remember me?"

The old man bent down and poked his head through the open driver's window.

"Wait, do you know this car?"

Clyde gripped the steering wheel and felt the familiar rush he used to get sitting behind it in his youth. The upholstery had seen better days. There was a lot of work to do. But this was his baby, and he would take care of her.

"It's taken me years to hunt her down," Clyde said, sliding the key into the ignition. "She was mine a long time ago, but I had to give her up. Now that I've found my way back to her, it's like I can start over again. You know what I mean?"

"I think I do, buddy," the man said. But Clyde wasn't listening. He turned the key and listened to the roar of the engine. The years had been kind to her. She sounded as young as ever. Clyde was falling back in love with Dahlia.

He killed the ignition and took one last look around. There was no doubt in his mind he was getting her back today. This would not be something he could walk away from. Clyde pushed open the door and stepped out. The man stood there with a grin on his face.

"Hey, since this car means so much to you, how about I knock off a hundred bucks?" The man said, smiling. "After everything you probably went through to hunt this car down, you deserve it."

"That's very kind of you. But would you mind if I checked one more place? I'm certain this is her. VIN number matches up and everything. But I want to be sure."

The man gave him a wink.

"I get it. Carved your initials in her somewhere or something like that, right?"

Clyde shrugged.

"Something like that."

He walked around to the back and slid the keys into the lock. This was the moment of truth. If what he was searching for was in the trunk, this was his car. He had no doubt he would find it. Better safe than sorry, of course.

The trunk popped open with a rusty creak. Most people would want to correct it. Clyde thought it gave the old girl charm. He loved her despite her flaws. Who wouldn't? He had spent so much of his life in this car. He spent time with his first date in Daliah. His first sexual encounter had taken place in the back seat. This car had given him so much and more.

Clyde stared down at the gray carpeting. Rust-colored stains spotted the fraying carpet, but that didn't matter much. New carpet would be easy to come by. If he decided to change it out, that was. There was something about leaving the car exactly as he found it that was endearing to him. The car couldn't change Clyde's imperfections, so why should he change hers? They had both grown older in their absence from each other. Time changed all things.

He reached in and tugged at the corner of the carpet. It took a couple of tries before it started to pull free. The old carpeting clung to the bottom of the trunk, desperate to hold on. The old man watched from over Clyde's shoulder with eager eyes. Clyde couldn't wait to show him what he had carved there all those years ago.

The carpet gave way and Clyde tossed it aside. He stared down at the familiar six-inch tally marks carved into the metal flooring. He heard the man grunt over his shoulder. He didn't understand what they were. Clyde would be more than happy to explain it to him.

"I take it that's how many women you've had in the backseat?" The man laughed. "Wait, that can't be right. There's only, what, twelve marks? With a car this sexy, you should be pushing at least twenty or thirty, right?"

Clyde shook his head and chuckled.

"It's not how many women I've been with." Clyde laughed. He pulled a small pocketknife from his pocket. A familiar rush had flowed through his body. "It's how many women died in the trunk.

Clyde turned to face the man. He felt more alive than he had in years. Something that had been missing from his life had returned. Clyde slashed the knife across the man's throat. The old man toppled over, clutching his wound.

Without wasting a beat, Clyde slammed the trunk closed and jumped behind the wheel. "Come on Dahlia," he said under the roar of her engine. "Let's go find lucky number thirteen." He shifted into drive and peeled off. The old man coughed and choked as the taillights sped away.

A Night Out

"This movie looks so real!" The woman in the car next to him shrieked. He wished they would put the top up. Danny didn't want to hear how impressed with the cheesy special effects she was. They were awful. What a stupid horror movie this was. Not only were the blood and guts cheesy, but the deaths made no sense at all.

Danny watched the man on screen lose his head in one clean sweep from a machete. It was old, rusty, and blunted. How could it chop through muscle, sinew, and vertebrae? It would take several whacks to cut through a human neck. Wouldn't that be more terrifying? To watch this killer chop away at the poor teen's neck until it was finally severed.

But the two young lovers in the convertible next to him ate it up. Each death was dumber and sillier than the last. Danny started to wonder if this was supposed to be a comedy. There was nothing scary about the movie. And that silly mask. Was the killer a hockey player? Danny couldn't follow it at all. What a waste of money this picture at the drive-in had turned out to be.

The girl in the next car over gasped again, but Danny missed what she had gasped at. He was no longer paying attention to the movie. His eyes had drifted down to his car dashboard. In his mind, he thought about what it did look like to behead someone. It didn't look anything like the movie at all. The familiar craving had risen in his gut again. His eyes lost their focus and the emblem of the galloping horse on the steering wheel became a blur.

"Greg, I have to use the bathroom," the woman in the car next to him said.

"And?" The man in the driver's seat replied.

"I don't want to go alone," she responded.

"What, are you scared? It's just a movie." The man laughed and the woman stormed out of the car in a huff. She flew past Danny's car and the aroma of her hairspray wafted by.

Danny knew an opportunity when he saw one. He waited a few minutes. When enough time had passed, he stepped out of the car and circled around to his trunk. To keep from gathering attention, Danny opened the trunk wide enough to get his hand through. Then, he pulled something free and stuffed it into his jacket as fast as he could. Without missing a beat, Danny headed off toward the bathrooms.

He made his way past the main building. A handful of patrons hurried inside, buying their concession as fast as possible. Behind the building, he found the bathrooms. A small light shone from under the bathroom door. He knew opening it would draw attention. If he was fast enough, no one would pay much attention.

With lightning speed, Danny ripped open the restroom door and slipped inside. Once in, he locked the door behind him. There were two stalls and a little sink under a dirty mirror. Only one pair of feet stuck out from the bottom of the stall. His prey was locked in with him.

He tip-toed across the tile floor until he was outside of the occupied stall. Danny readied the machete in one hand and prepared to kick open the door. Before he could, the door exploded into a burst of shrapnel and splinters. The force shoved Danny into the wall behind him. Towering over him stood the woman he had followed in. She looked different now. Her features were all distorted and grotesque.

Her mouth opened as wide as a snake's with teeth that grew into thin points like razors. The color drained from her face and her hair whipped in a non-existent breeze. Danny tried to let out a yell of terror, but the woman pounced on him. Her fangs ripped into the tender flesh of his neck. There was an audible gurgle as Danny tried to scream. Warm blood oozed down his chest and he started to feel cold. Then, darkness took hold of Danny.

When she finished her task, the woman walked over to the mirror and fixed her makeup. A drop of blood rested on her chin, and she dabbed it with a paper towel. Not a single hair was out of place. No blood rested on her chin. She walked out of the bathroom and back to the convertible. She slid in beside her boyfriend and rested her head on his shoulder, kissing his neck.

"I was hoping I took long enough in the bathroom that I would miss the rest of this awful movie. It's too scary for me." She hid her eyes by burying her face against his chest. Her boyfriend stroked his fingers through her hair and laughed.

"Oh, Barb, you're a silly woman," he said with a laugh. "I assume it's done?" He whispered in her ear.

She looked up at him and smiled.

"He's gone. Drained him dry. It will take them months to find the body in the ceiling."

"Great work my love," he said, licking his lips. "But next serial killer we stalk, I get to kill. It's not fair you've done the last two. I'm getting hungry."

The two shared a smile and settled in to watch the movie. The killer on-screen continued to murder his victims in the most outlandish ways possible. Barb continued to jump and squeal at the gory scenes. They did make her uncomfortable. Watching innocent people die always struck a nerve with her. But she never felt bad for killing and eating the murderers they hunted. They were the scourge of the Earth.

The Stall

It was dark and creepy in the gas station bathroom when I walked in. We had been driving for almost five hours and my bladder was close to exploding. The only gas station we found was a rundown-looking place off the side of the highway. It looked like it saw one customer a week, tops. But it was good enough for me. I told my husband to park right outside the bathroom door to make sure no creepy guy followed me in. I don't think I had been ready for the dirty surfaces and flickering lights, though I should have expected it.

I decided to use the larger stall. You know, the one meant to be wheelchair accessible? I wanted to spend as little time in this bathroom so the stall with everything in one would be perfect. I could pee, wash my hands, and run out of this bathroom. There was such a creepy vibe in there and I didn't like it.

The stall in the farthest corner was pitch black. The light above it had gone out and draped it in darkness. There was no way anyone would want to use that stall. I didn't understand why the attendant didn't replace the bulb. But I assumed women didn't frequent this restroom, so it was far down on his to-do list.

I stepped into the stall and placed one of those seat covers down. I'm not a germophobe, but the condition of this bathroom looked like a staph infection waiting to happen. Just looking at the metal surfaces made me feel like I would get tetanus. This vacation would not start with me getting sick because I couldn't hold it for another ten miles.

As I sat on the toilet and started to relieve myself, I heard a noise coming from the opposite side of the bathroom. I was certain it was the pitch-black stall. At first, I wondered if someone had been in there the whole time, but I remembered seeing the door cracked open. Would someone risk leaving the stall door unlatched? Unless the stall door was broken. That was possible in this filthy place.

But the sounds didn't sound human. More like a strange clicking noise. I would have thought some sort of bug or animal had nested in the dark stall, but it sounded way too large. The clicking echoed through the entire bathroom and started to grow louder. The noise started to freak me out and I wanted to rush from the bathroom. Unfortunately, I wasn't quite finished with my business. I tried to push harder, hoping it would help me pee faster. I just wanted to get out of this place.

The clicking stopped at the same time I finally finished peeing. I wiped and stood up as fast as I could. While I pulled my pants back up to my waist, I tried to press the flush lever down with my foot. Nothing happened. I pressed harder but it still wouldn't flush. I no longer cared if I left a mess in the bowl or not. The clicking sound had returned followed by a strange tapping. It sounded like a sharp fingernail on one of the stall walls.

Without bothering to wash my hands, I darted from the stall and headed towards the front door. Behind me, I could hear a stall door creak open and I froze in horror. Ever so slowly, I turned my head to glance behind me. From the darkened stall in the corner, I could see movement. Something tall, gangly, and pale crept out of the darkness. It wasn't a person or even an animal. At least, not like one I had ever seen. My hands shook at my sides as I stood there looking over my shoulder. The creature moved slowly on all fours. Its arms and legs sprawled out like some sort of four-legged spider. It had the features of a person, more or less. Arms, legs, torso, head. Each appendage twisted and bent in unnatural ways. Its face was nothing more than a gaping maw of teeth and a long tongue.

It had no eyes which meant it couldn't see me. The tongue flicked through the air like a snake's, and I realized it was tasting a scent in the air. It crept closer and closer to the stall I had come out of. Then the disgusting reality hit me. The urine still in the toilet had attracted it.

Even from this distance, I could make out the pinholes in the side of its head. No doubt they were ears. I didn't know how good its hearing was, but I was afraid to make a single sound. The beast was large enough to take two strides and be on top of me in no time. There wouldn't be time to open the creaking door before it pounced. I had to stand there and wait for this disgusting creature to enter the stall I had come from.

Drool dripped from the razor-filled mouth as it clicked its nails on the tile floor. My heartbeat hammered so fast in my chest I thought the beast would hear it and lunge. It stopped for a moment outside the stall and moved its face closer to the inside latch. I watched in disgust as its tongue licked the latch, leaving behind a sticky residue. Then, it proceeded inside the stall. From inside, I could hear disturbing sounds like a dog lapping up its water bowl. I held back vomit as I thought about that creature enjoying my urine as a treat.

I hoped the sound of the sloshing toilet bowl would cover my escape as I reached out for the door handle. When my hand touched the metal, the slurping stopped. I swear my heart stopped with it. The clicking noise returned and I realized something horrible. It had caught another scent. As fast as I could, I ripped the door open and flung myself over the threshold. I heard nails clacking on the tile as the creature ran towards the door. It let out a strange screech as the bathroom door shut behind me. A second later, I would have been dead. I was sure of it.

My husband was still sitting in the driver's seat of our car when I climbed in. He smiled at me as I buckled. "All better?" He asked. I looked in the side mirror at the bathroom door. The tip of the beast's tongue poked out from under the door and then retreated. I looked at my husband and nodded, hiding the shake in my hands. There was no chance he would ever believe me. And I didn't want him going in that bathroom to prove anything to me. I wanted to get as far away from this place as possible.

Cake

I know my coworkers hate me. It's no secret. None of them say good morning to me. Hardly do I ever get a passing glance in the halls. At lunch, no one talks to me. There seems to be a general disdain for me. I'm unsure why. I've not done anything to anyone. Usually, I stay at my desk and do my work. There's no time for silly office dramas. Work is for work. That's my belief.

I know I can't control their feelings and I can't change my ethics either. I'm not the social type. Though, I have tried to branch out a bit with my coworkers. It was brief, but I tried. Once, they planned an outing at a local bar. I thought it would be nice to grab a beer. Shortly after I arrived, people started to leave. Everyone seemed to have an excuse. "I need to pick up my kids", "My dog has been home alone too long", the excuses kept coming. Eventually, I was there alone.

One thing I've noticed about everyone in the office, they're rather trusting with the food they eat. There's this counter space, you see, which is designated for food available to everyone. If it's there, it's fair game. People bake whole dishes and place them on the counter. Almost everyone always partakes. That level of trust is outstanding.

Well, today I left a cake on the counter. I got here extra early to leave it out. There's already a group of people in there now, cutting it up and talking. But not for long. The poison works slow but it's fatal. I hope they enjoy the cake.

For Family

Family means everything to me. Family doesn't stop at blood. I consider close friends family. Even those married into the family. It's not only a word. It runs deep.

Imagine the sorrow I felt when I learned my brother-in-law, Liam, had been cheated on. He showed up at my door one night in a complete wreck. I felt for him. He told me everything. She'd slept with a coworker while on a business trip. There wasn't a more betrayed feeling.

I knew the feeling well. My last marriage ended in adultery. You never know when you're not going to be enough for someone.

Of course, I related to his pain and was able to make him feel better, even if it was only an iota. Since we were family, I told him he always had a place to stay. Liam couldn't stop thanking me for the support. I told him it was no big deal. That's what brothers were for. That night he crashed on my couch.

The next day, he was still just as upset. I couldn't blame the man. It's not something you get over right away. He started talking about how much he hated her and how he wished they'd never met.

That night, he came back to my house with a favor to ask. A big one. Liam wanted his wife gone. At first, I thought he meant out of his apartment. I was more than willing to drive her wherever she needed to go. He looked at me with a cold stare. There was real anger in his eyes. He hated that woman, I could see it. He wore it like a mask.

"Anything for family, right?" he asked.

I repeated the words back, afraid of what he meant.

Now, I can hear muffled cries coming from the basement. I'm sitting here with Liam trying to decide what to do. After all, anything for family.

The Schoolhouse

I went for a hike today on a mountain trail. It's near my home and I've never been down the trail before. In fact, I didn't even know it was there. I felt like taking a spontaneous hike today, so I drove around until I found a trailhead. One of the positives to living in the Smoky Mountains. There are trails everywhere. Every day could bring a new trail and not repeat for a year.

This trail sat on the side of the road, so I pulled my car over on the shoulder and parked. People do this all over here in the Smokies. You get used to seeing random cars parked everywhere. Usually, the trails are popular here and you see several cars parked. No one had parked at this trailhead this morning. I guessed I would be the only person hiking it today. Which was fine by me. I would get all the scenery to myself. Of course, I started to wonder if it meant the trail was a bad one. There was the possibility that it led to nowhere exciting or flooded out this time of year. But I didn't care. I would hike it no matter what.

I grabbed my hiking bag out of the trunk and headed down the trailhead. The dirt crunched beneath my boots as I walked. The rich aroma of mountain air and trees filled my nostrils. There was a brief hint of pine trees on the breeze reminding me of Christmas. The trip was already off to a great start.

The trail began to ascend the mountain. Roots crisscrossed out of the dirt forming what looked like a natural staircase. Having steps of sorts seemed easier than climbing a gradual incline. But I knew I would feel the burn in the morning. At the top, I stopped for a moment to retrieve my canteen from my hiking bag. Becoming dehydrated out here could spell danger for a hiker. There are so many trails, that someone may not stumble on you for hours or even days.

The path weaved around flat ground for a little less than a mile before it started its descent back down. In the back of my mind, I made a mental note that I would have to climb back up this incline on my way back. I wasn't looking forward to it. By the end of the trail, I would be tired.

After another half a mile or so, I found a small stream with a bridge crossing it. Well, I say bridge, but it was more like a fallen log. Someone had fashioned a thin log into a bridge. It was easy enough to cross but I could only imagine crossing it in the rain. It would be too easy to slip off. Luckily, the drop was only about two feet into a small stream.

Another mile or so later, I started to see something in the trees ahead. I had no idea what to expect at the end of this trail. Many trails here end at waterfalls so I was hoping for the same. But whatever this was looked man-made. I could see the outline of a wooden roof and walls as they appeared through the trees. It was a little peculiar. At first, I thought I had stumbled onto someone's property by mistake. Continuing forward, I made my way to a small clearing. Surrounded by vines and weeds stood a dilapidated cabin. Some planks appeared rotten and damaged. Others looked almost brand new.

I circled around the front of the building to find it had no door. Only a dark opening that resembled an open mouth. In my mind, I pictured a slimy tongue and sharp teeth. Inside the darkened building, I could see a few tables and chairs. With small steps, I approached the opening and peered inside until my eyes adjusted. Before me were little wooden desks. It looked like something from the 1800s or so.

I stepped inside to marvel at the old, wooden desks and chalkboard still affixed to the front wall. As I did, lightning cracked in the sky and made me jump. I could smell the ozone in the air. The bolt had struck close by. Then I smelled smoke. The lightning must have struck a tree. I rushed towards the doorway, terrified a forest fire would burn this place to the ground. Where there was no door before, one appeared. It slammed shut in my face. Smoke billowed from under the door and I could feel the heat radiating off the wood. I knew the building would burn in a matter of seconds.

All around me screams burst out and I threw my hands over my ears. They sounded like the shrieks of little children. I scanned the room, hoping to see some kids hiding in the corner but there was no one there but me. The schoolhouse groaned and creaked as it threatened to collapse. Sweat poured down my face as I searched for an exit. A voice broke through the schoolhouse like the wailing of an older woman. I turned to see the outline of someone flailing around in front of the chalkboard. Her invisible hand struck the chalkboard and scratched down with a terrible sound. The children's screams grew louder and I forced myself to move.

I pulled the hiking bag off my back and rammed it through one of the windows. The glass shattered and I leaped out of the building. A stray piece of glass sliced my arm, but the pain didn't register. I was glad to be out of that awful place. To my horror, when I turned around, the schoolhouse was gone. I Instead, there stood a brown sign. I glanced down at the words and read.

This sign marks the spot of the Norton Schoolhouse. It tragically burned down in 1881 after lightning struck a nearby tree. This plaque commemorates those who perished here.

The hike back to my car was a blur. I can't remember much after reading that sign. And I swear, I will never go down another trail as long as I live. I can't explain what happened to me, but I think I would rather forget it.

Getting Angry

I've been screaming for help for the past few minutes but no one in the house seems to care. You see, I'm trapped in my bedroom. The doorknob seems to be stuck. No matter how hard I try, it won't budge. It doesn't even feel as if the knob turns under the weight of my hand.

I've tried banging on the walls but no sound seems to come. I wonder if I'm going crazy. Why won't anyone come up here and let me out? Maybe something terrible has happened to the rest of them?

The window! Of course, why didn't I think of it sooner? Rushing over, I try to lift it open but it, too, is stuck. I try to signal a neighbor walking by with her dog. She glances up at the window but quickly looks down. I could swear she saw me but why did she pretend not to?

The sound of creaking stairs fills my ears and I hear talking, though I don't recognize the voices. Again, I begin to yell for help. They pay no attention and I can hear them enter a different room and continue talking.

Am I being held captive? Is this some sort of sick prank? That has to be it. My buddy Shay is a big prankster. He probably locked me in my room and now has friends over, telling them to pretend to not hear my yells. That crazy guy is always playing around.

"Alright, man," I call out. "You got me. Joke's over."

There's no response.

"Come on, man, this isn't funny. I've got shit to do today."

Again, there's no reply. I can hear the muffled voices in the other room. Pressing my ear to the wall, I can tell there are three of them, though I can't make out what they're saying.

Wait a minute, there's nothing in this room. That doesn't make any sense. This was my room. My furniture should be here. How could it not? Was it part of the prank? Did Shay remove all my furniture from my room? That would be impossible.

The voices have left the other room and heading for mine now. Thank God! They will let me out and this will all be over. I watch in suspense as the knob shifts and the door finally swings open.

"Here's the second bedroom," a female voice states as the door opens completely.

"Hello, thank God you opened the do-" I'm cut off by the second woman holding hands with a man.

"Oh, honey, this would be the perfect nursery."

"Nursery? No, no, no. This is my room. What the hell is going on? Where's Sh-"

Again, I'm cut off.

"It would be perfect."

I now notice the woman standing in front of the couple is a real estate agent. The couple smiles back and I could see her pregnant belly. They're trying to buy this house? But I'm in it still! I'm right here. Why are they pretending they can't see me?

"You've got to be fucking kidding me! Why are you guys ignoring me? Hello?"

I get right in their faces but they don't react at all. "What the fuck?" I ask.

The three of them turn and head out of the door. The real estate agent moves to close the door, threatening to trap me inside. "I don't think so," I yell, leaping towards the doorway. Nobody moves, no one flinches.

I have no idea how it happened but I landed in the hallway behind them. We should have crashed into each other. There should have been pain but instead, there's nothing. The man exclaims he felt a cold breeze but nothing more.

They carry on to the next room and continue to talk but I'm not waiting around to see what other terrible thing is going to happen next. I'm getting the hell out of this house.

I run downstairs and head for the front door. My hands slip off the knob and it doesn't budge. Again and again, I try with the same result. I try to cry but I don't feel any tears. I don't feel anything at all. There's no hot, there's no cold. I can't even feel the metal knob in my hand. Am I going insane?

Moving to the kitchen, I see a glass on the counter. I try to pick it up but again nothing happens. "Fuck!" I scream. This can't be happening to me. I try to push the glass with my finger and it wobbles only slightly. I try to push the glass for over five minutes and finally it moves an inch.

Whatever has happened to me might be finally wearing off. When the couple and the real estate agent come downstairs, I move back into the room. Waving my hands, I call out for them to look but they still don't see me.

I'm getting angry now. This isn't funny or amusing. These people are going to know I'm here one way or another. Heading back into the kitchen, I smack the glass with tremendous force. I watch as it sails across the room, smashing against the wall.

They heard that. Oh, they heard that indeed. If they don't acknowledge me now, they're about to hear a whole hell of a lot more!

I Found Willing Candidates

It's always been my dream. Ever since I was young, I would write short stories for my friends. They weren't any good but I was a kid, so my skills were lacking. As I aged, I assumed my writing would grow. It seems I was wrong.

My latest book was well received. There was only one minor problem. Almost every critic complained about the same thing. The violence didn't seem realistic. As a horror author, this is a terrible criticism to hear. I spent countless nights racking my brain for better descriptions. I watched a myriad of horror movies and tried to describe the violence. Nothing helped turn my scenes around.

Even the most brutal and horrifying deaths I wrote came off as campy. Nothing more than B-rated knockoffs. My writing seemed to lack a darker element which gave the violence life. As it stood, I felt I would be better suited for comedies.

Plot has always been my strongest skill. Countless reviews had commended my plots with five stars. So, why couldn't I nail the gore? What was I lacking and how could I get it?

I tried several "how-to" books and even a few writing classes but nothing seemed to change. There had to be a better way. I tried reading murder reports and browsing archives of infamous serial killers. I even visited a morgue to surround myself with death but nothing seemed to help.

Nearing a level of frustration I had never felt before, I decided to take a walk in a local park late at night. I figured a darker setting would spark a creepy description. I walked for hours with nothing but my cell phone flashlight to cut through the total darkness.

Large, cold raindrops began to fall and I craned my neck, looking for shelter. A few yards ahead, I found a small entrance to a cave that cut into the large hill in the center of the park. It was small but I managed to squeeze through. Once the storm was over, I would make the walk back home. To conserve my phone's battery, I switched off the flashlight and stuck it back into my pocket.

It took a minute for my eyes to adjust but when they did, I realized I could see. Not well, but enough to make out shapes. I had no idea where the light source was coming from. It may have been minimal, but it was enough. My curiosity couldn't be ignored. I gave in to my curiosity and moved farther into the cave.

Crawling on my hands and knees, I explored the cave. After an immeasurable amount of time, I realized I was lost. This cave system seemed to snake around for miles. But a quick look around told me I was closer to the light source. Everything had become brighter. There was a slight hum in my ears. When I rounded the next corner, I saw something I had never seen before.

A bluish cloud floated in the middle of a vast space before me. It hung several feet in the air and trailed downward, touching the ground. I climbed to my feet and stared at the blue, pulsating mist. It hung there like a curtain and my curiosity burned once again. Venturing forward, I placed my hand inside. Pulling it back, everything seemed to be fine. Too many horror stories had me believing there would be monsters inside, ready to devour my flesh.

My knees shook as I stepped forward, pushing my face into the cloud. Inside, I saw a new tunnel. It was unlike any I had ever seen. Without a second thought, I stepped inside. It was lit up with a blue color, yet I saw no lights. It seemed as if the tunnel, itself, was the source. It stretched on for what seemed an eternity. As I turned, I noticed something impossible. The tunnel moved with me. No matter where I looked, there seemed to be a tunnel, and yet there was only one. I stood for a long moment, trying to understand the bizarre sight before me.

When the queasy feeling in my stomach subsided, I began to walk. Whichever direction I chose to walk, the tunnel appeared to follow. Though I could see only one path everywhere I looked, it seemed as if there were hundreds to choose from. Eventually, I saw another misty cloud before me. Wasting no time, I plunged inside. The world around me was now bright and sunny. Somehow, I had found my way out of the cave. Thinking I had crawled around all night, I pulled out my phone to check the time. "No service," blinked on my phone's screen before it died.

After several minutes, I was able to flag down a lone hiker and asked for the time. “One in the afternoon,” she said, looking at her phone. It was impossible. How could I have explored all night and all morning? I wasn't tired at all.

"Are you okay?" She asked, watching my confused expression. Shaking out of my daze, I looked at her.

"Sorry, I was lost in the caves all night. Feeling a little lightheaded," I told her. She smiled at me.

"Do you need to borrow my phone to call someone to pick you up?

I took her up on the offer and pulled the phone from her hand, calling my closest friend. If anything, I needed to talk to someone about what I'd seen in the cave.

"Hello?" He answered.

"Tim, buddy, it's good to hear your voice. Listen, I got stuck in the caves down at Cedar Park all night. Do you think you could come down here and-"

"I'm sorry, but do I know you? He cut me off. I laughed it off, thinking it had been a stupid joke but he wasn't laughing.

"Sorry, I think you have the wrong Tim," he said and hung up. I looked down at the phone as if it would help me understand and what caught my eye made my blood turn ice cold. The date listed the current month as October. But that couldn't be possible. It was May, wasn't it? Somehow, I had traveled five months into the future. But why hadn't Tim recognized me? Then, like a semi-truck, it all hit me. The strange tunnel, the missing time, everything. This wasn't my world. Somehow, I had traveled to a different world. Another reality. It was unbelievable. I had so many questions, so much I wanted to know, and things to explore. But an idea flooded my mind. There was a way to fix my writing and it was right in front of my face. I looked back up at the woman and smiled, thanking her for her phone.

I can tell you now, my writing is getting better. I've been able to describe the horrors in my writing more eloquently. The screams, the panic, the gore, the violence. It all seems so...real now. And I'll never forget the woman who lent me her phone and started it all. She had been the first of many I brought back to my world for practice. After all, I have a whole world filled with people to practice on now.

Medical Transport

Chris drove through the desert on a long stretch of dark road. His eyelids had begun to feel heavy, threatening to drift him off into a deep sleep. Road trips were better taken with other people. Having someone to talk to when his eyes felt heavy made all the difference. Music and podcasts were no longer enough to keep his brain active or his eyes open. The lack of streetlights and other cars on the road gave him nothing to focus on.

Chris drummed his fingers on the steering wheel as he tried to keep himself awake. Music played over the speakers at such a low volume he had to strain to hear it. Which was fine with him since he had listened to almost his entire music library now.

He tried to preoccupy his time by looking at the night sky. It was far enough away from any major city that the light pollution didn't disturb the sky. He had seen this view many times before, but it never ceased to amaze. It looked like a sheet of lights across the sky. Pinpricks of light covered almost every inch of darkness. It made him feel small and insignificant in a good way.

Stargazing only worked for so long before his eyes began to grow heavy again. Chris shook his head, trying to stave off the fatigue. He knew it wouldn't work but grasping at straws was all he had.

Up ahead, he saw the soft haze of red taillights. They lit up like a beacon on the horizon. It was unusual to run into another car this far out. At least there was something to take his mind off the exhaustion for a while. He came up with all sorts of stories for this other car. Where they were coming from. Where they could be going. Who was driving? And why? He came up with several fun backstories to help fill his mind.

His favorite was a creepy thought. It was a serial killer prowling the long stretch of road, looking for his next victim. Of course, that would mean Chris was in danger. But he played out a whole scenario in his head. First, the would-be killer would try to run him off the road. Chris wouldn't go down without a fight. He would avoid the chaotic driver's rams. Like any good horror movie,

Chris' car would break down at the worst time and cause him to pull over to the side of the road. The killer's car would roll up to him at a slow and menacing pace. With there being only desert on either side of the road, there would be nowhere to get out and hide. Chris would have to fight his attacker head-on.

The taillights grew brighter and snapped Chris from his daydream. He realized he had been pushing the gas harder than he meant to and had now caught up with the other car. It turned out to be nothing more than a white van with the words Medical Transport on the back. This intrigued him more than the idea of a serial killer. What could be in the back of that van? Was it organs being transported to a hospital? Or a cadaver headed to a university?

Chris decided to fall back a few yards and let the medical transport gain some distance. He didn't want to ride on his bumper, nor did he want to pass yet. The driver was going over the limit already so there would be no reason to pass.

Having someone to follow seemed to ease his drowsiness for a while. There was something to focus on now. He kept the back of the medical transport van in the center of his vision. The van seemed to decrease speed. Chris found himself catching up without driving faster. If this kept up, he would pass the van for sure. He wasn't going to drive under the speed limit out on this stretch of open road.

Something moved in the back of the medical transport van. A dark figure, nothing more than a shadow. But Chris was sure he had seen something. He was almost certain these vans didn't transport people like an ambulance. Or did they? Either way, his curiosity had piqued. He wanted to know what was in the back of the van.

Chris pressed the accelerator down a fraction of an inch. He wanted to gain speed, but not at an alarming rate. He preferred to gradually catch up to his target. As he approached, he could see there was something in the back moving around. Though, in the darkness, it was impossible to tell what it was.

From his current position, he couldn't see much. Something was moving around in the back, but it was nothing more than a shadow. Chris decided the best way to get a good look would be to pass the medical transport van. He pressed the gas down farther and pulled the wheel to the left. As he accelerated, he glanced over at the van to get a good look inside.

For several yards, Chris stayed even with the medical transport van. Something shot up from the darkness and pressed against the inside window of the van. A charred hand pressed against the glass. Skin peeled back exposing white bone. The hand seemed to bang against the glass like it wanted to escape. The driver paid no attention to the commotion behind him.

Chris honked his horn and flashed his lights to get the driver's attention. He continued to stare forward like he was in some sort of trance. Before Chris could try again, a face pressed against the glass and smiled. It was the most hideous creature Chris had ever seen in his life. It looked human but twisted and distorted like a meat pretzel. The burned skin clung to its face as it thrashed around in the back of the van. He was so startled by the encounter, he jerked the wheel and spun out into the sand.

His car slid to a halt with his headlights facing opposite the direction of the van. He stared into the darkness of the desert for a moment, clearing his head. Then he craned his neck to see the medical transport van slip into the distance. Chris took shallow breaths until he was finally calm. What he had seen in the back of that van had made no sense. Was it a burn victim? If so, why the medical transport? Wouldn't he be in an ambulance? None of it added up. He could only hope the late-night drive had caused him to hallucinate.

Writing on the Stall

I've always been fascinated by the random writings on bathroom stalls. So are a lot of people. At least, they must be because I have a few thousand Instagram followers. All I do is share stall art and writing. My handle is @amyinthebathroom. Sounds like a porn site, I know. It's the best I could come up with.

I've seen all kinds of things in bathroom stalls. I once saw a damn good copy of Starry Night. You know, the Van Gough painting? I've seen dragons, cats, presidents (usually in promiscuous and mocking situations), and more drawings of penises than I could ever count. What's the fascination with them? Jesus. Oh, one time I read the exclamation "Make love, not war" to which a clever individual responded with "Give me your number and I'll start right now."

I guess people have a lot of free time while taking care of business. I think it's great. Of course, because of my growing Instagram page, I find myself in crappy bathrooms a lot, no pun intended. I've seen everything you could imagine. Gloryholes (which are disgusting), hook-up requests, political rants, phone numbers, and the ever-not-so-clever message of "For a good time, call Jenny. 867-5309." Haha. Good one. No one has ever done that before.

But, it's the message I'm currently reading now that has me writing this blog post. That's right guys, I'm on the John as I write this. Get over it. ;) To be honest, though, it's got me a little creeped out.

Picture this. A run-down gas station in the middle of nowhere. The bathroom looks like it hasn't been cleaned since Nixon was in office. What makes me think that? For one, there is a newspaper clipping in a frame on the wall with the headline "Nixon Resigns" So yeah...

Anyway, there's a creepy message on the stall by my head. It reads, "I'm tired of doing this dance. It's not worth it anymore. Today, I end it all and you're coming with me." Now, I know what you're going to say. And you're probably right. It probably is just a troll. But the creepy part is, the writing looks fresh. Like it's still drying. And now, I'm hearing footsteps a few stalls over. No, I'm not joking. As soon as I publish this blog, I'm running for my car. I'll let you know as soon as I'm safe. Wish me luck.

The Fountain

There's this fountain near my place of work. I like to spend a lot of my lunch breaks there. It's a serene place to relax and enjoy a stress-free session away from the hectic office life. If I could somehow do all my work while sitting next to the fountain, I would. Unfortunately, I'm still required to return to the office every day.

Today, something happened during lunch that I couldn't explain. There was a strange noise coming from the fountain. Like a low hum. Not a mechanical hum but something...human. I approached the fountain and looked down into the water. Ripples broke across the surface from the churning fountain, but I could still see clear to the bottom. It appeared empty.

Still, the humming continued. I thought I was going crazy. Something in the water was making noise and I couldn't see it. The pitch began to rise and fall in a sort of melody. Now, I knew it wasn't mechanical. Something, or someone, was down there.

An impulse came over me and I dripped my face into the water. Liquid filled my ears but so did the humming. It was clearer now. The distinct rise and fall of a melodic voice were clear. After several seconds, an image began to appear before my eyes. The bottom of the fountain was no longer visible. In fact, neither was the fountain. Instead, I found myself in a large body of water like the ocean. It was impossible. My feet still stood on solid ground but all around me there was nothing but open water.

This was only the second strangest thing I saw beneath the surface. Beings swam here and there, calling out their beautiful song. They were women, of sorts. My first thought turned to mermaids but that wasn't quite right either. They looked beautiful with the upper body of a woman. Their lower half was long and serpent-like. Not the scaly fish-like tails I would imagine a mermaid possessing.

One of them approached me and stared into my eyes. She sat there for a moment and I became lost in her bright, blue eyes. Though she didn't speak a word, I knew exactly what she wanted. And I would give it to her.

I lifted my head out of the water and looked around. The fountain was as it has always been and I could see nothing below the surface. Resisting the urge to peer back beneath the water, I went back to work and about my day. While I sifted through work emails and expense reports, my mind could only focus on the fountain. I needed to see it again. I needed to see them again. But I knew there was only one way of doing so.

Heading off to the breakroom, I started chatting with one of my coworkers. I told him how I saw this cool thing swimming around the fountain. An otter, I claimed. But I knew this was a lie. It didn't matter. I needed someone else to go to the fountain with me and if I said I'd seen mermaids, they'd have me committed.

He grabbed his phone so he could snap a couple of pictures of the cute animals and we went on our way. When we arrived, the fountain looked as it always had. Nothing out of the ordinary. But I knew better. They were still down there. I could still hear the hum. It still sounded like a beautiful song. And I would join that song soon.

When my coworker said he couldn't find any otters, I told him he would need to look closer at the water. He pushed his face within inches of the surface. But I needed it closer. Grabbing the back of his head, I held his face underwater. His muffled screams told me he saw the beings. The humming in my ears grew louder and louder until finally, my coworkers stopped moving.

A hand came out of the water and pulled the body beneath the surface. I wanted to look but I knew what my purpose was now. The beings required more sacrifices. Humans are their food, but they couldn't leave the water. So, people like me are chosen to bring it to them. Of course, they don't live in the fountain. I'm not sure where they are. But they can open a portal of sorts through the water. All they need from me is deliveries every week. And I've got an office full of people who will do just fine.

New Year, Same Me

Once the clock strikes midnight on New Year's Eve, people wipe clean their slates and start fresh. New year, new me, they'll proclaim. Of course, it's all hyperbole, but with good intentions. And I suppose I'm not one to judge. I'm guilty of it as well. This year, in fact.

You see, I'm an addict. My resolution was to break my addiction and clean up my act. I'm tired of living my life with these controlling urges for a fix. I see others living a clean and healthy life and I want that for myself. A simple resolution was all it would take. A promise to myself to cut free from the shackles of addiction. I could do it. I would do it.

The first week went well. No urges, no relapse, no thoughts of addiction. For the first time in my life, I believed in the new year, new me mantra. And it felt good. Liberating, in fact. If I could break my addiction cold turkey, I could do anything.

The second week got harder. Urges would come and go. I had to concentrate hard to keep from relapsing. Proud of my self-control, I went about my life. But things weren't as easy as they had been the week before. Little things upset me and I found myself with less patience than before. But even this was manageable.

When the nightmares began, I started to come undone. Waking up every night in a cold sweat was enough to drive anyone crazy. But I knew this was part of the withdrawals. "This too shall pass," I told myself. Only it didn't pass. It got worse.

Soon, I couldn't eat, I couldn't focus, and I couldn't sleep. I would hallucinate in the middle of the day. Even though I had no food in me, I would vomit every morning. Mostly painful dry heaves for fifteen minutes. Tremors set in, my teeth began to chatter, and my feet started to tingle. I tried to fight through it all. I was going to beat my addiction. This was a new year and things would be different.

"But we both know how this story ends," I say aloud to my audience of one. "In the end, I caved. I gave in to my addiction." I sit up in my chair and smile. "After all, that's why you're here," I say and stare down at the crying woman chained to the floor. She thrashes and moans through the gag. God, how I missed this. "New year, same me," I say as I pick up the knife and twirl it through my fingers.

From Santa

Christmas morning is always a special time for kids and parents. The little ones rush out of bed and spot the presents under the tree from Santa. Parents relax while watching their wonder-filled children unwrap gifts from a mythical being.

For Laura and Logan, this particular Christmas was a sad one. Only a couple of weeks before Christmas, their father had walked out on them and their mom, Kylie. The siblings were too young to comprehend why their father had left. Their mom always did her best to keep things quiet. She needed Christmas to be perfect.

In reality, she was a broken woman. She hadn't slept since Daryl left. And for what? Some whore of a woman who would likely cheat on him before the new year? Kylie couldn't understand. She had loved him with all of her heart. How could he do this to her? Christmas was her favorite holiday. Hadn't he known that? Or did he not care?

There was one cure for her sadness. Watching her children sit on the floor next to the beautiful Christmas Tree. They sifted through the boxes, trying to figure out which of the presents they would open first. Laura and Logan read the tags and made piles of their presents.

"How about that big one in the back?" Kylie called out to Logan. "I'll bet Santa left something really special in that one."

"Ok," Logan said as he dragged it from under the tree. It wasn't overly huge, maybe the size of a cake box only a little taller. Logan, as most kids do, gave it a nice shake, eager to know what was inside. He found no clues in the sound.

"Go on, Logan. Let's see what Santa got you." She smiled at her son and he began tearing at the paper. Bits flew everywhere and his little sister collected them in a small pile behind her. She looked pleased with herself as she watched her older brother.

Logan revealed a cardboard box and placed it on the floor. A bit of red wrapping paper still clung to the bottom. He held back the urge to roll his eyes at the sight of having to open his gift for a second time.

"Go on, son. What's inside?" Kylie encouraged him. He peeled the tape with his fingers until it finally came free. With excitement and anticipation, he flung open the cardboard panels.

For a moment, he stared inside the box, not sure what he was looking at. His mother smiled down at him. He looked up at her and no longer recognized the face that looked back. Her smile had changed from happy and joyful to twisted and sinister.

"What did Santa give you, Logan?" She sneered but he still wasn't sure. He reached in and pulled at the item inside. It rolled over with a sickening *flop!* And Logan let out a blood-curdling scream.

"Merry Christmas, Son."

Logan jumped up and pulled his sister by the hand. He dragged her out of the house and into the snow. He cried as he led a confused Laura to a neighbor's house and told them everything. When the police finally arrived, they found Kylie in her bathrobe, sitting on the couch. She held in her lap the severed head of her ex-husband. She ran her fingers through the mangy, blood-soaked hair and hummed Christmas carols, ignoring the police as they approached.

Another Day at the Office

There has long been a rumor that our office building sat atop an Indian burial site or something to that effect. I'm a lifelong skeptic of the paranormal. So, all the stories about ghost sightings in the bathroom late at night have never bothered me. I've worked late several times and never saw anything creepy or out of the ordinary. Except for Brenda picking her nose when she thinks no one is looking. God, she's gross.

Everything changed when some local news station caught wind of the possible graves. All it took was one small little news story and *bam!* The people wanted the injustice rectified. A private business couldn't sit on top of unmarked graves. It wasn't right. Or so said the news. To keep rumors from spreading, the owner decided to have archeologists investigate. He never thought they would find anything.

Well, I'm sure you can guess what happened next. They came out to our office building with ground-penetrating radar and walked all over the place. Leaving at the end of the day was a nightmare. We had to wait for the workers to clear a path so we could drive out of the lot. Always holding up the traffic. But they found something. It wasn't proof of graves, but something was buried down there.

Over the next couple of weeks, there were diggers on site sifting through the dirt until they found what they were looking for. Sure enough, there were a couple of graves buried in a small grassy field next to our building. I wish the archeologists hadn't disturbed the graves. They were better left alone.

I've lost track of how many days we've been trapped in this building now. Something won't let us leave. Whatever those archeologists did disturbed something. I can no longer say I don't believe in ghosts. I've seen them with my own eyes now. They haunt this building. They are keeping us here.

Sometimes, we find someone's body tucked away in the darkest corner of the building. The look on their faces tells us they died of intense fright. I can only imagine what sort of paranormal horrors they experienced in the dark.

I'm left wondering what happens to their soul when they die here? Is it trapped with us? I'm afraid I'll find out soon enough. When it's my turn to die of fright.

Imagine living in a haunted house all day, every day. If horror is your thing, that might sound like fun. But I assure you, it isn't. I've watched co-workers commit suicide because they could no longer stand the constant ghostly torment. There are voices down every hallway. Shadowy figures in every corner. Lights flicker on and off. Disembodied hands will reach out from the darkness and grab you or scratch you. It's a nightmare we can't wake up from.

The outside world has forgotten about us, it seems. I've glanced out the window and never see another person on the property. Cars drive by on their morning commutes without a single head turning our way. How could a whole building of people be forgotten about overnight? Our work phones won't connect. Cell phones have no signal. And the internet doesn't work. There is no way to contact the outside world. These spirits have trapped us here.

I watched Brenda hang herself the other day. She had a strange gleam in her eye and an excited smirk on her face. I don't know if it was possession or happiness to end the suffering. These spirits seem to take pleasure in torturing us to death. I've been wondering lately, who they were in life. I can't help but wonder if the cemetery was lost for a reason. I think it was a whole cemetery of horrible people who did awful things in life. Some sort of murderous cult. But I'm sure I'll never learn the truth.

This never-ending torment must stop. I can't stand it any longer. There' are so few of us left, now. Some have dropped dead of hunger or thirst. That's how long we've been trapped here. You would think the hauntings would become commonplace, but they don't. It keeps ramping up. The spirits are less physical now and more in our heads. We have visions and dreams of horrible nightmarish things. I feel constant pain and anger. Have they possessed my body? I'm not sure...

I'm leaving this note on the receptionist's desk in the hopes that someone will find it one day and know what happened here. I'm sure whoever reads it won't believe it. I sure as hell wouldn't. It all sounds made up. I know. But believe me. This happened to us all. We have all been trapped in our office building for what feels like months. There's no chance of escape. Our ghostly guards won't ever let us leave. So, there's only one way out and I'm taking it today. I guess Brenda had the right idea long before me. At least now I understand why she had that creepy-ass smile. It's the only freedom from another day at the office.

Through the Monitor

It's late at night and I'm extremely tired. But when a baby cries, you have to check up on them. Right now he is crying. I can hear his screams through the baby monitor on my nightstand. Reaching out, I grab the receiver and press the button to see the video feed. Now I can see him flailing around in his crib, an upset look on his face. There's no chance he will be going back to sleep.

Sitting up in bed, I fling my feet over the edge and stand up. A quick stretch and I head to the kitchen to prepare a bottle. His cries echo through the dark and lonely house. My wife is not home tonight. She's been working hard lately and taking care of our son. I told her to go out with her friends tonight and get a drink. I guess she had a few too many and ended up staying at her friend's house for the night. It's fine. I think she deserves it.

As I shake up the bottle, my son screams louder. It's almost like he can hear the bottle being made. Or maybe he senses it. Who can say? Either way, I want to quiet him down and get back to sleep. Taking care of a child by yourself is tough work. I find myself thinking about single parents and can only commend them.

Heading back towards his room, I crack open the door and slip in. It's dark in here but my eyes adjust within a few seconds. There he is. There's my beautiful boy writhing around in his crib. I find it funny when he gets so angry for a bottle. He acts like someone is trying to suffocate him. But the noise is piercing and I want it to end.

Scooping up my son, I stick the bottle in his mouth and try to quiet him with gentle rocking. Carrying him to my bedroom like a basket of eggs, I prop myself up in the bed and watch television while he snacks. I don't dare look at the alarm clock on my nightstand. I don't want to know how late it is.

He begins to slow down and his eyes shut. I know he's getting ready to go back to sleep but I must burp him first. This is the part I hate. Not because I'm afraid to hurt him but because I know it will wake him.

He begins to fuss again and I put the bottle back in his mouth. As I do, a familiar noise comes from the baby monitor. At first, I'm confused but then the hair on the back of my neck stands up. I can see the image of my child's room on the monitor. There is no one in there. Yet somehow, there is a cry coming from the monitor. A cry that sounds exactly like my son's. I look down at my baby but he is sucking away at his bottle without a care in the world. I am unsure of what is waiting for us back in that room.

The Glass Box

I thought I knew what hell was, but I was wrong. Hell is this place I find myself in now. You see, I'm trapped in this small, glass cube. I have only enough room to stretch out my legs and hardly enough room to stand. How do I breathe? Not sure that's much of a problem here. I'm certain I'm already dead.

When I said this place was hell, I was being literal. I think I died and went to hell. From all the stories, I thought hell would be a dark and scary place filled with demons and fire. It seems the opposite. All around me, people are happy. The sky is bright and blue. It's a cheery and wonderful place. Except for this damn glass box. But I suppose that's the true hell, isn't it?

I'm forced to sit here and watch the life I wish I could be living. Everyone else is happy around me. I want out of here so bad. I kick and I push but nothing ever budges. Even worse, there's a hammer on the other side of the glass. I could smash this box to pieces if I could somehow reach it. But to do that, I need to be out there. I'm trapped.

Oh, I haven't told you the best part. There's a man whom I'm certain is Satan. He walks by with a smile on his face and a skip in his step. Every day, he asks me how I'm doing. My answer is always the same. I tell him I want out of this dreadful place. I want to be free. He smiles at me and says, "I know you can get out of there someday." These simple words do nothing but bury me deeper into this metaphorical pit I find myself in.

Why couldn't I have been buried in a coffin beneath the ground? Why not trap me in a small cage far from the light of day? Why must I endure the torture of seeing a world around me I can never live in? One that I want to be a part of. What kind of sick hell is this?

The people here, if they are people at all, are awful. They smile and wave at me as if nothing is the matter. Several ask how I am but never wait around to hear the answer. No one cares how I'm doing in here. They're all glad they're not in the box. And the hammer is right there. Any one of them could set me free but they choose not to. And I've begged. I've cried for someone to smash the glass with the hammer and set me free. But the answer is always the same. "I wish there was something I could do to help." With that, they keep walking.

I want to die in here. I want this glass prison to be my coffin. But if I'm already dead, this will never happen. Instead, I'll be doing this for all eternity. That I simply can't take. There's no way to know how long I've endured this torture already, but I can't take it for another moment. And yet, there's no way out. I'll spend the rest of eternity slamming my hands against the glass and begging those who walk by for help. They will ignore me, I have no doubt. But if I slam my hands long enough, I may see a crack.

My New Haunt

"If you'll come this way, sir," the apparition said as he sauntered towards another house. The name tag on his somewhat see-through label said, Pierce. "This is a wonderful home. I am sure you would be quite happy spending your eternity here." I looked up at the Victorian-style home before me. The old iron gates, the giant windows, and the marble statues gave it a cliché horror movie vibe.

"I don't know, Pierce. This house looks haunted, you know? I don't think I want to live in a haunted home. People would be expecting that. I want something modern. You know, new design. Maybe a young family."

Pierce nodded and scribbled notes on a pad. "Of course, sir. I understand. Right this way." A door materialized from thin air and he pushed it open. Having been recently deceased, this was all very new and strange to me. But I decided to roll with it. Hell, what's the worst that could happen? I was already dead, after all.

Before us stood a beautiful home with an elegant and modern design. It was square and full of windows that reached from the ceiling to the floor. A pathway led to the front steps surrounded by ponds and plants. A rich family lived here, that much was clear. This seemed like the kind of place I could stay.

"You'll find this has everything you're looking for. Modern design, many rooms for haunting, a rich and stable family. You'll be able to kick back and spend the rest of eternity haunting up a storm and you'll do it in modern luxury!" His sales pitch was well-practiced and convincing. I hardly needed to see the home before I decided I would take it.

"Excellent choice, sir. You're going to be so happy here." He pulled a paper from a briefcase and handed it over to me. "If you'll just sign this paperwork, we'll be all set." I laughed as I realized something. Buying a home in the afterlife was much simpler than buying a home while alive. There was no fine print to the contract, no hidden fees, nothing. The contract stated I could move in immediately with full access to the house for haunting purposes. The contract was only void if the family were to successfully expel the spirits from their home. Otherwise, the place was mine.

In life, I had never been a homeowner. I could barely afford the studio apartment I was living in. My minimum wage job didn't provide much. The afterlife doesn't have these restrictions at all. I don't need a job, pay isn't required, and anyone and everyone can own a home. I guess my Earthy body truly was a prison.

Lockdown

The whole damn city is on lockdown right now. I've never seen anything like it. We can't leave our homes even for a second. They say there's a fast-spreading virus out there. It's the most contagious disease they've ever seen, and it kills about ninety percent of infected hosts.

Currently, my town is ground zero. I don't think it has spread beyond our area yet. Which is why the army quarantined us. They believe they will cut it off at the source but I'm not so sure. If it's as contagious and lethal as they say, then the only way to keep it from spreading would be to kill us all. Though I'm sure they're currently weighing that option.

Despite the lockdown, people still sneak out. And I can't blame them. Sitting at home for hours with nothing to do gets boring. And before you say watch TV or browse Facebook, I should tell you these services have been cut off. They even blocked the cellular signals. We barely have running water or electricity. Both are being rationed. Armed soldiers in hazmat suits drop off boxes of food on our doorsteps each week. We're to wait twenty minutes before collecting to ensure the soldiers are well out of harm's way. Every so often, there is the faint sound of gunfire as a citizen opens their front door too early.

Since we can't see the news here, I assume what's happening here isn't being reported around the country. At least, not the full story. I doubt the American people know we are being shot dead for venturing out of our homes. Then again, maybe they do, and they're fine with it. Anything to stop the spread.

I can smell the aroma of burning flesh almost every day as they burn the dead. They're hoping it will stop the spread but it's not working. Which probably explains why we're all still alive. Even after the corpses have been consumed by fire, they're still contagious. Killing everyone would solve nothing. They would have to dissolve each of us in acid to stop the spread, I would imagine.

The interesting thing about this disease is, not everyone in town is infected with it yet. It seems to only spread from person to person contact and doesn't linger in the air long. Which isn't unusual, I suppose. But what *is* unusual is how contagious it is. The virus isn't airborne but being around a person for even a moment is contagious. Masks do nothing to save people. Hazmat suits don't even work. It's almost like the virus spreads by sight. Hence, the reason for the lockdown. We aren't even allowed in the same house as other people. Families were torn apart in the early days. What they did with those they took, I don't know. I suppose the infected were killed.

As for the symptoms of the virus, well that's complicated. No one knows the full range since we're so cut off from each other. All I know is there are two categories of infected. Those who die and those who don't. Those who get it but don't die seem to continue to be contagious. Even after they get better. It's baffling. As for those who die, well it's different from person to person, it seems. Some go peacefully in their sleep while others scream and puke up blood. No one case has been alike.

But enough about the virus. I want to talk about myself. You see, I'm one of the ones who got infected but didn't die. I made it through the symptoms and survived. Of course, I'm sure I'm going to die here in this town. The government is going to eradicate us like pests. I can feel it. In fact, after making it through this I feel...different. Stronger? I'm not sure what the right word is. But something is different.

I think this virus does more than infect and kill its host. I think it changes you if you survive. I'm still in the early stages of my recovery so I don't know anything for certain yet. What I do know is, I have the urge to infect others. This thing in me wants to spread and I want, no I need, to help it.

This brings me to the other thing I wanted to tell you about. I found a way to sneak out of my house in the middle of the night. The military has no idea. What do I do with my nights out, you ask? Well, that shouldn't be too difficult to figure out. I told you, this virus wants to spread. As do I. So, I've been visiting neighbors while they sleep. They get infected and I move on. It's not clear yet how many of them have died or overcome it. But in the next few weeks, we'll know. And one thing is for sure, when there are none of us, they won't be able to stop us. And that's why I'm here in your room with you, talking to you while you sleep. In the next few days, you will either be part of our army or burned by theirs. Sleep tight, my friend.

Come Back to Me

The table spread out before me was a platter of breakfast food fit for a king. Eggs, hash browns, toast, coffee, grits, pancakes, and much more. I could smell the delectable aroma and my mouth began to water. Had I been able to move my arms, I would have dug in immediately. My stomach roared in protest from the lack of nourishment over the last few days. I had not had a single thing to eat in three days. And water, only a few sips. My mouth was so dry I could almost feel the cacti sprouting up over my tongue. I spotted a large glass of orange juice on the opposite side of the table and I hung my head. All this was nothing more than a tease. I wouldn't be able to eat or drink any of it. How could I? My arms and legs had been zip-tied to the chair.

I had no idea how I had come to be in this place. I woke up here a few days prior. From what I could gather, it was a basement. It's all I knew. The first day had been spent calling out for help and trying to find a weakness in the chair and ties. I found none. A masked person came in once a day to give me a small bit of water. Enough to keep me alive, I imagine. It was cruel. It was horrible. Worst of all, I didn't know why it was happening.

As I wondered if I could somehow rock my chair forward to grab even a small piece of bacon in my mouth, the basement door swung open. I expected to see my masked captor standing at the top of the stairs as usual. But not this time. I didn't expect to see *her* again but, there she was. My ex-wife. My mouth hung open in awe. Until this moment, I believed it was an action only done in books. Here I was, doing it myself.

She sauntered down the stairs, swinging her hips from side to side. It was almost hypnotic. She smiled at me and sat across the table, taking a long gulp of orange juice. "What the *hell* is going on," I shouted. Again, she smiled and slid a piece of bacon into her mouth. I could almost taste it myself. God, I was hungry.

"You were a naughty boy, Hugh." She picked an apple from the table and took a bite. "You left me and found a new woman. That really broke my heart,

Hugh." I stared at her in confusion. We had divorced years ago and I had moved on with my life. Wasn't that normal? Isn't that what everyone did? None of this made any sense.

"Just let me go, Maria. I don't know what it is you're doing here but-"

She picked up a knife and shot to her feet. As she walked around the table, she let the blade drag across the wood. With two delicate fingers, she picked up another strip of bacon, only this time she held it out for me. Without hesitation, I gobbled it up. The taste was remarkable. My stomach growled in exuberance. I then watched as Maria slid the knife under the ties around my arms and cut them loose. "Eat up," she said and walked out of the room.

There was no hesitation. I ate everything I could get my hands on. Like a savage, I stuffed the bacon and sausages into my mouth and washed it down with a mix of coffee and orange juice. I found steak mixed in with the eggs and ripped it apart. When I finished, the table looked like a hurricane had swept through.

Maria once again opened the door and trotted down the stairs. She stared at me and the mess with glee. I wondered if she had poisoned the food and decided I didn't care. I'd rather die than stay down here any longer.

"So, how was she?" she asked. Utter confusion clouded my mind. Was she asking me how the sex with my current wife was? What an odd thing to- Then it clicked. I looked at the table of demolished food and cried. I tried to vomit but nothing would come up. Maria giggled and came closer, pulling her phone from her pocket. She swiped her finger across the screen. I saw images that made me feel faint and nauseous. There was Maria, carving up my wife, Casey, like a fucking Thanksgiving turkey. My blood boiled under my skin. Maria tilted her head back and cackled. "Ready to come back to me?" she howled.

I took no time grabbing the steak knife from her hand and embedded it under her chin. She gurgled and choked on the blood now spurting from her neck. Her eyes grew wide and she looked down at me in disbelief. I could see the life draining from her eyes as she took a small step back. I reached out to snatch the knife back but I missed and she tumbled backward to the floor. A pool of crimson seeped out from under her body. I screamed in frustration and panic. I tried to kick my legs free with all my might, but they would not break free.

It's been days since all this happened and I've not been able to get free from this chair. The god damned thing is bolted to the floor and I have nothing to break the ties with. I can feel the weakness setting in and the stench from Maria's rotting flesh will soon become unbearable. I'm writing this for whoever finds my body. I want the world to know what happened here.

Watcher

He had been seeing it for weeks, now. That same mutilated face that stared at him with its twisted, lipless smile. Crooked, rotting teeth pointed every which way. The unblinking face and bulging eyes only ever stared at him. The being never spoke, nor did it seem to threaten. It only watched.

Everywhere Josh went, the watcher stayed with him. There was no escape from it. In the shower, it would peer over the top of the curtain and watch him. In the car, it would sit in the back seat. At work, it would stand in his cubicle.

Josh tried to attack it on several occasions. His fists would phase through its body like it was made of mist. No one around could see it, either. It was his own personal demon. One he could never escape from. He would run around corners to get away from it, only to see it standing there waiting for him. It never spoke. It never moved. It only watched.

After weeks of dealing with this thing, he needed it to end. There was never a moments peace from it. It was enough to drive him mad. He thought about seeing a doctor. Maybe he had gone crazy. But seeing things that weren't there was a good way to end up in the mental hospital. He couldn't fathom the idea of being locked in with *it*. There was only one way to get away from it now.

Josh sat in his seat on the plane as it traveled through the air. His watcher stood in the aisle next to him, staring. The flight attendant walked by pushing the drink cart out in front. She and the cart passed right through the watcher.

"Excuse me," Josh said, waving her down. "I've changed my mind. I think I'll have that drink after all."

The flight attendant smiled and poured him his Coke and Whiskey. The liquid poured down his throat, burning his throat. If he was going to conquer this thing today, he wanted to calm his nerves. He could think of no better way than with alcohol.

His watcher looked down at him with its unblinking stare. Its body was taller than any normal being should have been. Its head scraped against the ceiling. It had to bend forward to fit inside. Josh knew from experience it could change its size to fit where it needed to. Anything to watch him.

He didn't know why or how he started seeing this thing. The first encounter had almost given him a heart attack. No matter how fast and far he ran, the watcher was there waiting for him. He screamed for help in a crowded street, and everyone stared at him like he was crazy. He couldn't blame them. He felt crazy.

Josh closed his eyes and sipped his drink. He didn't want to see the twisted face any longer. He could sense it, still. Even through closed eyes, he could tell it was there watching him. The cold stare bore a hole in his head. He could almost feel the heat of it.

"Jesus Christ!" he yelled, opening his eyes. "Why can't you *fucking* leave me alone?"

The other passengers looked at him in surprise. No one knew who he was screaming at. A couple people pulled out their phones, ready to record whatever came next. Josh was sure to give them a show they wouldn't forget.

"I'm sick of you watching me you ugly piece of shit!" he screamed as he stood and tossed back the last bit of drink.

"You're there when I wake up. You're there when I take a shit. You're there when I try to crank one out! What do you get from watching me, huh?"

He threw his empty cup through the watcher. It bounced off an elderly woman's head behind it. Josh paid it no attention. He was ending this here and now.

"Please, for the love of God, everyone. Tell me you can see this twisted mother fucker." He pointed at his watcher, but no one seemed to react. He felt that if he could find one other person who could see it too, he would feel better. He would be validated. If it was real, then he wasn't crazy. And if he wasn't crazy, he could find a way to kill it.

"Sir," the flight attendant said. "I need you to return to your seat."

Josh grabbed her by the arms. There were gasps all around him.

"Please, ma'am. Tell me you see it." He pointed at the smiling figure beside him. He could have sworn the smile grew wider.

"Sir, you need to take your hands off of me and take your seat, now." She spoke with a firm and commanding voice. This was not her first time dealing with unruly passengers.

Josh scoffed and let her go but he did not return to his seat. Instead, he pushed past her and headed towards the front of the plane. Standing in front of everyone, he started to cry.

"Please, one of you must see it. I can't be the only one. I'm not crazy. I'm not! It's always there, watching me. It won't leave me alone. I can't be its show anymore. Whatever it wants with me, it can't have it!"

All the faces on the plane were looking at him now. Several phones pointed in his direction, waiting for what would come next. His watcher stood there staring.

"Fuck this," Josh said as he rushed the door. Before anyone could stop him, he had pulled the release handle. The door flew open, tearing at the hinges. Josh tumbled out of the plane with a gush of air. Oxygen masks dropped from the overhead compartments as the plane plunged several feet. People screamed and cried in their seats before the plane stabilized.

Josh fell through the air with a sound rushing past his ears like a roaring waterfall. He looked around and did not see his watcher. It seemed the air was one place it could not follow. Below, the ground was fast approaching. He knew it would be down there waiting for him, but he no longer cared. He was almost free.

Right before he hit the ground, Josh had time to notice there was nothing but an empty field waiting for him. His watcher was nowhere to be seen. His last thoughts were of peace. He had finally found a way to be alone, if only for a few minutes.

On the plane, a woman struggled to calm her nerves as she breathed through her oxygen mask. After a few moments, she noticed something at the front of the plane. Every time she blinked it drew closer until it stood over her, staring. She let out a scream and glanced around but no one seemed to notice it. It stood there watching her with its twisted, crooked smile.

The Embers

The Beast

I know it's out there somewhere. Not even sure what *it* is. But I watched the creature lunge from the water and take my father overboard. That was seventeen years ago, now. Today, I begin the hunt for the beast that took him from me.

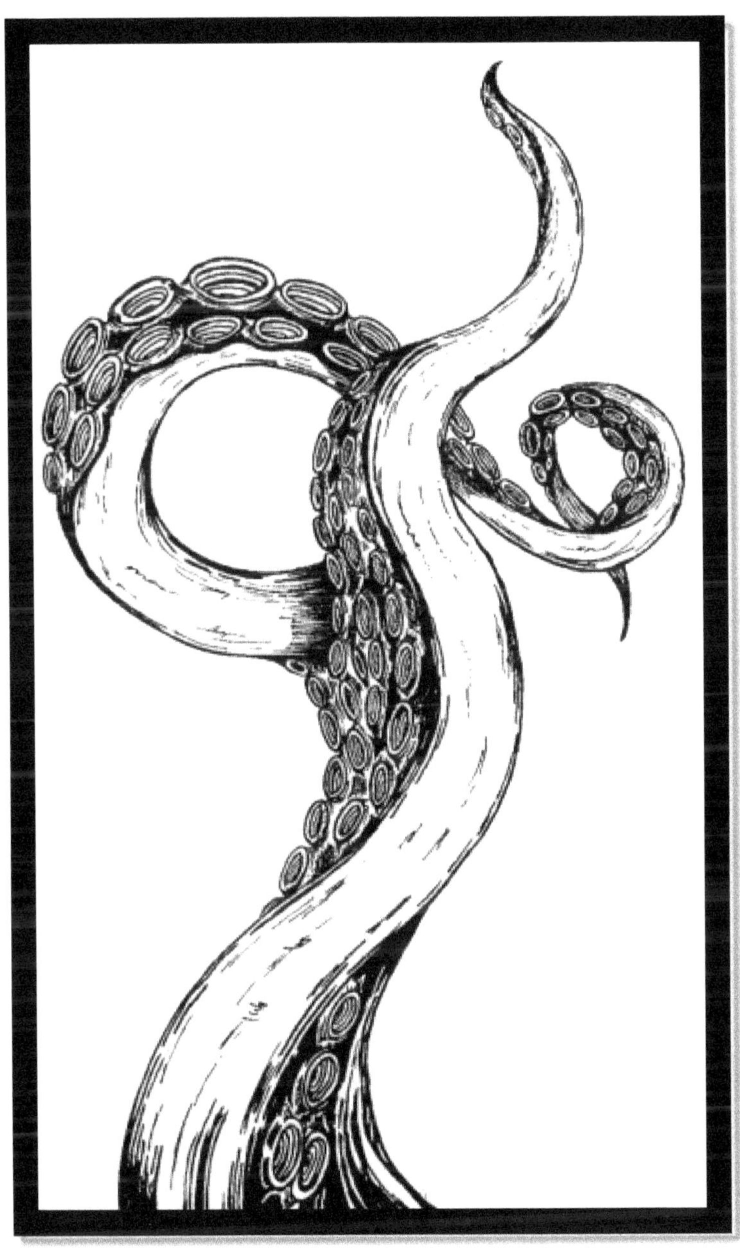

Pool with the Devil

"It's just a game of pool," he tells me. "It's not a big deal. If you win, you'll get a lot of money." I ask him what if I lose. "Well, I would highly suggest you win, of course. Otherwise, I keep your soul." He laughs and I wonder why I ever agreed to play pool with the devil.

The Wall

While exploring a new place, I found a small town with a wall around it. My curiosity got the better of me, so I hopped over to see what was there. But there is no way back over. And the smell is horrendous. Like rotting meat. And the growls coming from the houses are unsettling.

Drive-In

Some say the old drive-in theater down the road is haunted. They say that because of the brutal murders that took place there almost a decade ago. The killer was never caught. Today, I was rummaging through my father's things after he died and I think I may have found the killer.

Path to Hell

They say the path to heaven is a staircase, but you never heard about the path to hell. Well, I can tell you it's awful. It's a winding boardwalk through the most horrible forest there is. All sorts of creatures and monsters trek through the woods and I'm certain every one of them wants to eat.

Out of the Smoldering Embers

Fire can be a destructive force. It mows down trees, buildings, animals, and anything in its way. But it can give life, too. Out of the smoldering embers of this fire crawled something small, yet terrible. Yet to be classified by science, but it would bring mankind to its knees.

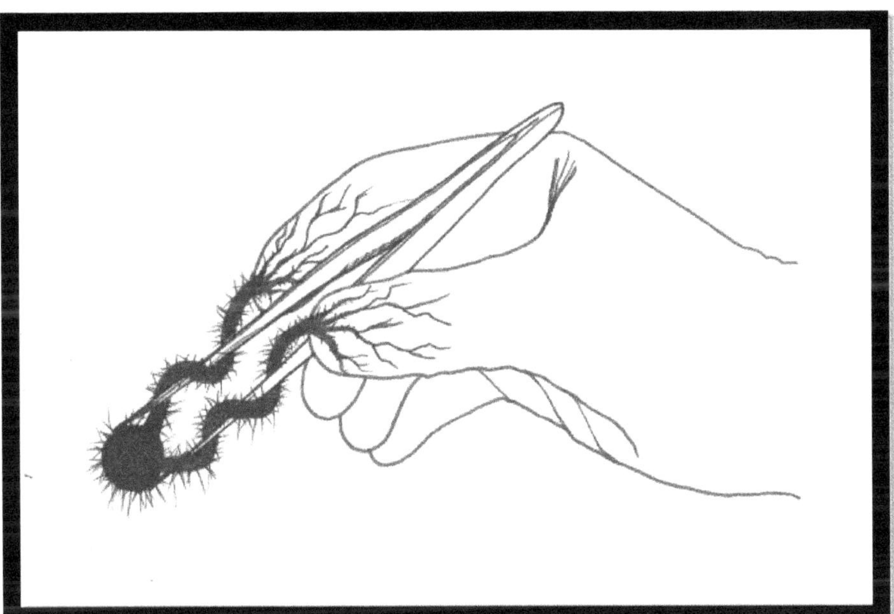

A Cold One

There's nothing like enjoying a cold one on a warm summer afternoon with a friend. The cool beverage slides down my throat like a log over a waterfall. I look at my buddy slumped in his chair and laugh. He slipped something into my wife, so I slipped something into his drink. And I know just where to bury the bodies.

POISON

Burial

When my wife past, I found the perfect spot to bury her. A small clearing in the middle of the woods. She had loved the forest so much. It only seemed fitting she would be buried in it. Of course, the police had asked what had happened to her. I only shrugged and said I didn't know.

Horror Movies

I was in the middle of watching a horror movie when the lights flickered. It was funny at first. The lights danced and came back on several times. But when the lights went out completely and I heard noises all around me, I began to get scared. That fear only heightened as my phone flashlight wouldn't turn on and something kept touching me in the darkness.

The Cabin

There's a cabin on the top of a mountain somewhere in the heart of America. It may look peaceful and beautiful. But I assure you, it's anything but. I feel sorry for the poor bastards who finally stumble on that place. The mess of bodies I left behind was revolting.

Flower Garden

The flowers grew beautifully this time of year. Rick admired them. His new fertilizer was working wonders. Now, he simply needed to find more drifters.

Walk in the Woods

Every once in a while, it's nice to get away from the city and explore nature. It helps to decompress from modern-day life. Things are quieter and slower in the woods. And it's so very peaceful out here. I just wish for once I could enjoy a nice walk in the woods without dragging a body.

Happy Couple

I watched this couple on the beach at sunset. They looked like they enjoyed their time together. For their sake, I hope they leave this beach before the darkness falls. I've got that itch again and it would bae shame to have to kill the happy couple.

Leap of Faith

Most people get an odd sensation of fear when looking down from high places. Not Daniel. No, he got the strange urge to leap. Not because he was depressed but because he was certain he could fly. He would never truly know until he took that leap.

Make it Home

The snow crunches under her feet as she makes the long trek home. It's freezing outside and the bitter cold bites at her limbs. She barely feels it anymore. Instead, she's focused on the gaping wound in her stomach. Her only thought is to make it home in time.

The Cloud

At first, it looked like a cloud in the sky. Merely, a summer rainstorm rolling in. When the cloud started to morph and shift in unnatural ways, people stopped and stared. Finally, the cloud descended upon the onlookers. As fast as it had appeared, the cloud was gone. So, too, were the people it engulfed.

Voices

I'm not sure where this tunnel leads. I found it one day in the farthest point in a nature park. It seems to go on forever. But I have to go back and explore it. When I first looked inside, I heard shuffling and a young boy's cry out for help!

Just a Movie

I always thought it was just a movie. The whole killer car plot seemed too fantastical to be real. But I found out the hard way. It's as real as can be. I've been trapped inside this vehicle from Hell for three days now. And whenever I try to leave, it runs down another victim.

Dream Car

Dennis finally got his dream car. All his life, people told him to work hard and earn his way. Why bother? It was much easier to stick the lifeless corpse of the previous owner in the trunk.

Dinner

Campfires are so mesmerizing. The way the flames flicker and dance in the night sky is wonderful. And the campfire smell is soothing. It's the best way to cook a meal, in my opinion. And soon, my meal will be done cooking. It's a shame my friend Donny won't be around to taste it. But he'll be at dinner all the same.

Cruise

Cruises are an excellent way to relax and a fun way to travel. My wife and I are taking one for our anniversary. It should be a lot of fun. And the best part is, they will never find the body. The ocean is so huge, after all.

Police Car

As I sit in the back of the police car, I start to question my decisions. It probably was a bad idea to get behind the wheel after having those drinks. But as the squad car flies past the police station and the officer driving ignores my yells, I start to worry about my future.

POLICE

Abandoned

My friend and I found an abandoned apartment complex. It was a lot of fun climbing the crumbling stairs and making our way to the roof. But as we looked out over the empty field around the decrepit building, we noticed something unsettling. Cloaked figures stood all around, staring up at us. I don't think this place was truly abandoned.

Halloween Decorations

I love Halloween. It's my favorite time of year. The creepy movies, the scary decorations. It's all great. This year will be extra special. One of my yard decorations, an old woman hanging from a tree, is going to blow everyone away. Partly because it's real.

Bathroom Stall

I've been stuck in this bathroom stall for over an hour. I just can't leave. There's something in the bathroom pacing back and forth and I think it's waiting for me. I don't dare glance over the stall either. Whatever it is has been growling my name the whole time.

The Basement

My parents told me to stay out of the basement when I was a kid. I was always too scared to go down there so, I listened. Now that they are both dead, going through their personal belongings falls to me. I had to step foot down there. I wasn't prepared for the hundreds of glass containers housing replicas of me.

Survival

She could hear the screams of people behind her as the fire engulfed the building. Many of the voices she recognized. Fear kept her from turning back to help. She knew people would call her a coward, but she knew the truth. It was survival.

The Town

I don't recognize this town anymore. Not because people moved away. Not because new stores have opened. It's the bodies. The hundreds of bodies that litter the streets.

Monsters

There's a monster that lives under beds. It protects people from the monster that lives in the closet. But the monster that lives in the closet protects people from the monster under the stairs. But all of them are afraid of the monster that watches people in the shower while they wash their hair.

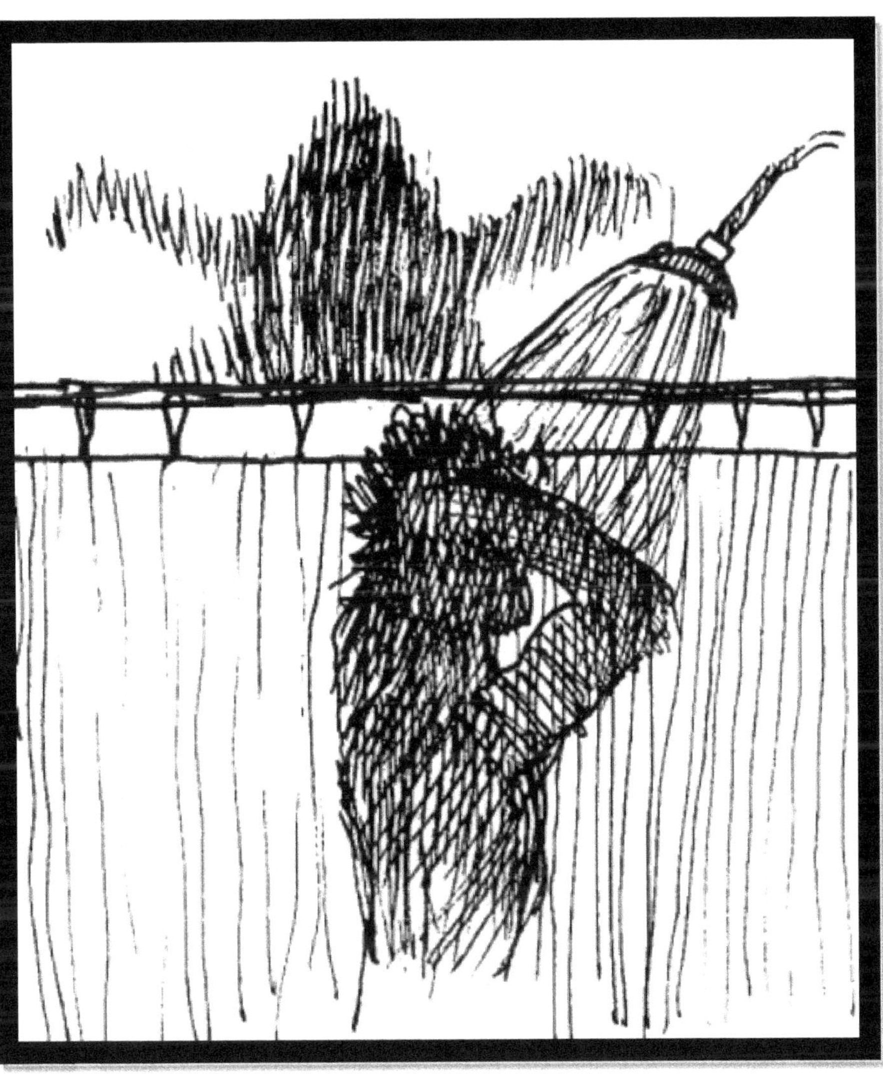

Web Cam

For fun, I checked out a website that allowed you to watch people's webcams without their knowledge. It was fun and exciting until I witnessed a murder live. Before I could call the police, the killer held up a sign to the camera. My name was written in blood and the word next.

NEXT!

Texts

There's this strange number texting me every week. I keep deleting it because I don't know who it's from. They keep sending me a strange combination of numbers. 1262, 1249, 1136, and so on. It wasn't until today I realized they were home addresses. The one they sent me today is mine.

1237
2456
1947
1624
3652
1237
1237

Message in a bottle

I found a message in a bottle once. At first, I was excited by the possibilities. Could it be someone lost at sea? Maybe someone from a different country? Excitedly, I unwrapped the parchment and read it quickly to myself. My blood ran cold as I read the words detailing my exact location, right down to the color socks I was wearing.

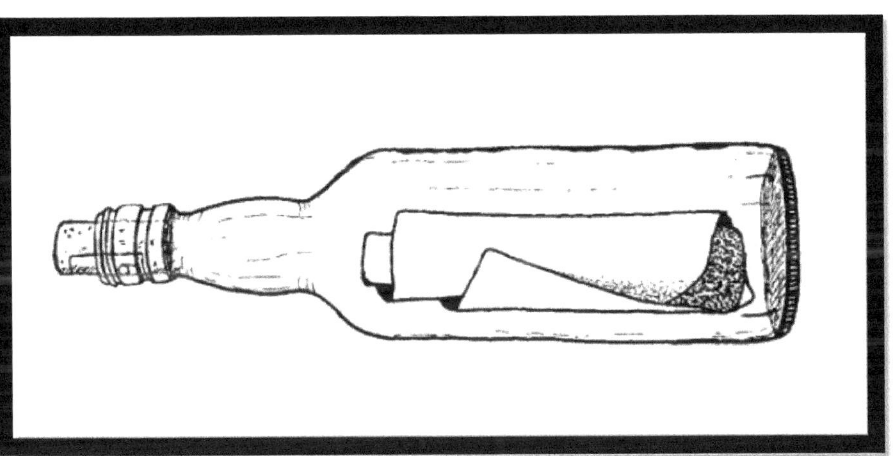

Writers

Writing can be a lonely profession. The author sits in a quiet room with nothing but their thoughts as company. But those ideas come from somewhere. Sometimes, the dark and twisted ideas don't come from their minds but the dark entity whispering into their ears, unseen.

Insignificance

As I stare down at the world below me, I feel a sense of insignificance. The world is a huge place. The universe is an even bigger one. But these thoughts are quickly pushed away as the creatures begin to tear the place I once called home apart. We are safe here on the space station, but we won't be for long.

Old Fort

There's an old fort in my town. Tourists flock from all over to visit. It was built over five hundred years ago. While exploring it the other day, for the thousandth time, I found a metal door I had never seen before. Something inside snarled and banged against the metal and I ran. I don't think I'll go looking for it again.

Train Tracks

There's a set of train tracks in town that don't show up on any maps. I can't figure out what they are for. But one day, I caught the train that uses it. There were several large box cars attached. The shrieks and moans that came from inside seemed otherworldly.

Theme Park

I have this great idea for a theme park. It would be horror movie themed. The patrons would have to survive the night in a horror movie scenario. So far, the test park has been great. The only problem is, no one has survived to tell their friends about it.

I'm Ready

My neighbor across the street never comes out during the day. I think I've only seen him out at night. He might have a night job and sleeps during the day. But he also acts afraid of the sun. I know it may sound crazy, but I think he's a vampire. We will find out today. I've got my stake and I'm ready.

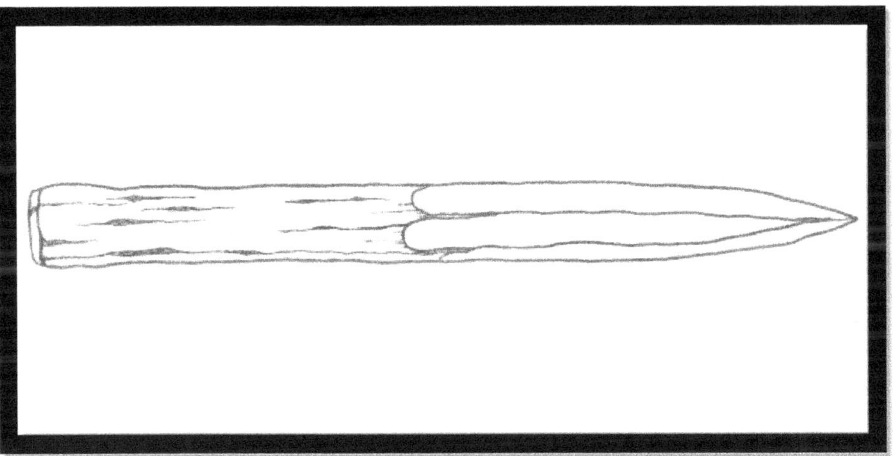

The Flames

Out of Room

She stood on the wooden dock staring out at the wide river before her. A thick fog had rolled over the surface of the water. The land on either side was no longer visible, hidden behind the veil. There was a chill in the air, but Helen did not seem to mind. Instead, she watched the current slip from beneath the dock and disappear into the fog.

Helen couldn't remember how she got here. It seemed the only memory in her mind was this dock. There was no fear at this notion. Only peace. She felt a sense of calm. The dock and the river weren't scary places. They felt like home.

An overwhelming urge to sit on the dock and dip her feet in the water overcame Helen. Without hesitation, she did just that. Removing her boots, Helen sat down at the edge of the dock and slipped her feet beneath the glassy surface.

The water was cold. Far colder than she had anticipated. Still, she did not mind. Helen let the current run past her feet. A cool massage. Something brushed the underside of her foot and she let out a soft laugh. She imagined a lone fish nibbling at her soles. There was no thought in her mind to pull her feet from the water. This place was tranquil and happy like a painting. No harm could come to her here.

Another brush to the underside of her feet made her leg twitch with laughter. A ripple emanated from her foot and traveled down the river. It disappeared into the fog. Somewhere down the river, a sound caught her attention. It sounded like water lapping against the hull of a small boat. Helen climbed to her feet and peered through the fog, trying to see.

The unmistakable sound of a paddle caressing the soft water echoed from somewhere inside the cloud. Something was rowing towards the dock. Helen waited with bated breath, wondering who else was here with her. She had not expected to see anyone else in this lovely place. But she was eager to see who it might be.

From in the fog came a wooden boat. The bow curled up towards the sky into a dagger-like point. A single lantern hung from the end, slicing through the fog. At the stern stood a large figure cloaked in black. He moved a large wooden paddle under the surface, propelling the craft forward.

As it came to rest at the end of the dock, the cloaked figure turned towards Helen. It did not speak and it did not beckon her. It merely waited. She could see no defining features of the figure. His body seemed to be made of the burlap cloak he was wrapped in. Still, Helen did not fear this figure or the place she was in.

"Am I dead?" she asked. There was no response.

In her heart, she already knew the truth. And yet, this did not frighten her. The sense of calm she had felt still clung to her like wet clothing. Water slapped the side of the boat in a rhythmic beat as the ferryman waited. Helen wanted nothing more than to climb aboard and sail down the river to whatever afterlife awaited.

As she stepped forward, ready to place a foot in the boat, the ferryman stretched out a single arm. There was no hand protruding from the sleeve and yet somehow she knew what it was signaling. She was not to step inside the vessel. The cloaked figure held out an invisible hand as if waiting for something to be placed there.

Helen was unsure what it wanted. An offering of some kind. A memory or a story she had once heard fluttered in the back of her mind. The ferryman escorted spirits from one world to the next. He required something to complete his task. An offering. But what?

She patted her pockets and heard a soft jingle. There was something in them. Dipping her hand into her right pocket, Helen produced two silver coins she had not been aware of before. They were unlike any coins she had ever seen. Two silver circles with unfamiliar markings rested in her palm. Helen outstretched her hand, offering them to the ferryman. His cloaked sleeve reached out. The fabric engulfed her hand and up to her forearm. When it withdrew, the coins had vanished. It now beckoned her to climb aboard.

A tingle of excitement surged through her body now. In life, the notion of death was not a happy one. Here with the ferryman, everything seemed right. It was natural. It was no more fearful than being born. Merely a next step in the journey of the mortal soul.

As the boat glided across the smooth river still shrouded in fog, Helen glanced down at the water. She could see a reflection of stars and galaxies inside the river. She craned her neck to look up at the sky, but it was cloaked in fog. Looking back down, she realized these were not reflections. This was the cosmos.

"It's like the river of time!" she exclaimed in wonder.

Everything that ever was or will be was in the river. Time, space, life, and death all resided here. Helen could not help but wonder if the answers to all of life's questions rested at the end of the river. She couldn't wait to learn what the afterlife was like. Which religion had been right? Her hands shook with excitement.

The stars and the galaxies began to fade from view. Now the river was black. There was no reflection on the water. It was a river of eternal abyss. Helen couldn't help but wonder where they were. She could see nothing around them still. The once beautiful fog now felt like walls closing in around them. The feeling of happiness and wonder melted away. Fear began to rise in her throat. An inexplicable change had occurred. One that she could not explain.

"Ferryman, where are we going?" she croaked. He did not answer. She pulled on his robe, hoping to gain his attention. He did not speak, nor did he move. "Please, answer me," she pleaded, reaching for the oar. Her only hope was to take the paddle away and keep them from reaching their destination. Perhaps she could paddle the boat back to the dock and return to her life.

But the oar would not budge. The ferryman continued without so much as a second glance at Helen. It seemed he did not even notice her presence. The overwhelming feeling of dread continued to rise in Helen. The urge to jump overboard and swim back to safety almost overtook her. Before she could act on her feelings, she tried to reassure herself it was all right. She had nothing to fear.

And what had she to fear? The ferryman had not told her where they were going, nor did she have reason to believe it was somewhere bad. It had been the stars and the galaxies. Losing their light had sent her into a panic. There was no reason to believe it was an ill omen. Instead, she told herself they had moved beyond time and space now. They were somewhere else.

The fog began to dissipate. She could see again. Except, there was nothing around to see. The shoreline was nowhere to be found. It seemed they were no longer on a river but instead had found their way into a calm sea.

The ferryman stopped rowing and stood still. The boat coasted to a stop against the laws of physics. Even without an anchor, it no longer moved. They did not bob on the current as she would have expected. Instead, they sat completely still.

"Ferryman, where are we?" Helen asked, peering overboard once more.

She saw screaming and bloated faces in the water now. Their arms outstretched towards the surface, begging to break through. A sea of fingers wiggled below the surface. She remembered placing her feet in the cold water earlier that night and thinking a fish had nibbled at her. Now, she knew better.

Helen could hear gurgled cries for help as the people below the water struggled for freedom. Despite the water rushing into their lungs as they inhaled, not one had passed out. It seemed they had become immortal in their time of agony.

"Ferryman, I-" Helen said, turning towards the cloaked figure. Before she could finish her sentence, the ferryman tipped the boat enough to throw her off balance. He seemed unaffected by the lateral change, but Helen slipped over the side and into the water. Before she could struggle to swim back to the surface, hundreds of hands wrapped around her and pulled her down.

She was now even with the faces of the drowned and immortal victims. Many tried to use Helen to clamber towards the surface. None could get closer no matter how hard they struggled. The ferryman peered over the side of his boat, looking into Helen's face. She let out a muffled scream and reached for the cloaked figure. Water rushed into her lungs, burning like daggers. Still, she survived. Mouthful after mouthful, Helen choked on water as she continued to breathe. Each time the water entered her lungs, she felt a white-hot pain. Her lungs burned for fresh air, but she could give it none. Within a few seconds, Helen had become like those around her. Screaming and struggling to get to the surface.

The ferryman pulled away from the water and stood still for a moment. A ripple broke out across the surface. Another soul had arrived for it to ferry. And like the others, the ferryman would have no choice but to abandon this soul in the water. The afterlife had run out of room, but the souls kept coming.

The Tree Trunk

His head was swimming in confusion with eyes lost in a fog of haze. Donny's arms felt glued to his sides; the rope bindings biting at his skin. Though he was bound, Donny was still upright. His back was pressed firmly against something. A pole or something. He couldn't tell. His senses had not fully kicked in from whatever drunken haze he had awoken from.

"H-hello?" he stammered. His mouth dry like it was stuffed full of cotton. "Is anyone t-there?"

He heard something crunch in the distance like the sound of boots on leaves. Now, he was beginning to understand where he was but not why he was there.

"W-why am I tied to this tree? W-what's happening?"

The only response, besides the silence, was that of the soft coo of a bird somewhere far off. Under his palm, Donny could feel the bark of the tree. It crumbled away as he dug in his nails, desperate to break free. He tried to kick but found his feet were tied to the trunk. Donny thrashed for some time before tiring himself out.

Another twig snap echoed through his ears. He glanced around with tear-filled eyes. His vision drifted from the haze until his surroundings became clear. He could see the forest around him, though it was still covered in a milky-white film in his eyes. Despite his best efforts to blink it away, the haze remained.

"P-please, if this is some kind of joke, it's not funny."

One more crack off to the right made Donny crane his neck. Stepping out from around the trunk of a tree was a man dressed in all black. His two gloved hands each gripped a different tool. In his left hand sat a crowbar. In the right, an ax.

"Hello, Donny," the man-in-black said in a smooth tone.

"W-who are you?"

"Not someone you wanted to see this evening, I assure you," the man replied.

He stepped towards Donny, brandishing the items like a salesman.

"We've got two choices here, Donny. Which would you prefer? Ax or crowbar?"

"H-huh?"

"The ax is good for chopping, but it makes things go by too quickly. The crowbar is good for smashing things. *Reeaaal* painful."

"P-painful? I don't know what you-"

"Excellent choice, Donny. Painful it is!"

The man-in-black swung the ax towards Donny and buried the blade into the bark above his head. Donny let out a yelp as he ducked his head down as far as it would go.

"Don't worry, Donny boy. Fun is only getting started."

Before Donny could contemplate the meaning behind the words, the man swung the crowbar with both hands. The metal connected with Donny's left ankle. He heard a loud *pop* and *crunch* as pain rocketed up his leg.

"Fuuuuuuuuck!" he screamed. "W-why are y-ou d-doing this?" Tears rolled down his cheeks. He had to fight the urge to crane his next down to see the wound, scared he would see a bone sticking out of the skin.

"Sorry, Donny. This is not the part where you ask questions. This is the part where you only suffer."

There wasn't another moment's hesitation. The man swung again, this time connecting with the right ankle. The bones crunched underneath the crowbar. Donny was afraid his foot was no longer attached. Another scream of pain erupted from his lips. It echoed through the trees. He could only hope somewhere off in the distance a lone hiker would hear his pleas and call for help.

"Yikes, that doesn't look good. Mangled your feet pretty bad. Don't worry too much about it. Nothing a visit to the ER and a few months of physical therapy can't fix. That's why I'm taking the knees, too."

"What? No!"

But it was too late. The man swung the crowbar in rapid succession, busting both kneecaps. His legs throbbed with pain. Donny knew that if the ropes were not keeping his legs fastened to the tree, they would be pointing in the wrong direction.

"There we go. You might never walk again, Donny. Ain't that great?"

"Y-you fucking psychopath!" It was all Donny could manage to say through the biting pain.

"Let's see. Ankles? Check. Kneecaps? Check," he said, miming the action of checking things off an invisible list. "What's next? Oh! I know. How about..." He trailed off and placed the tip of the crowbar against Donny's crotch.

Donny shook his head violently, pleading with the man to stop. Sweat poured down his face, hiding tears. His pants were soaked with what he believed to be a mixture of blood and urine. There wasn't much feeling in his legs other than excruciating pain.

"Maybe we'll save that bit for later, huh?"

The man wasted no time swinging the crowbar again. It connected with Donny's right hand. It was crushed under the force. His fingers bent and curled in different directions. Donny cried out in pain, surprised that he could still feel anything. He had thought his body would have grown numb to the pain by now.

He felt the cold metal touch his left hand. Donny looked up into the eyes of his attacker and saw burning hate there. More than anything, he wanted to plead for the man to stop but he knew it would be useless.

"Tell me why I'm doing this, Donny, and I'll leave this hand alone."

"Please...don't," Donny choked.

"I'm sorry. Is that please don't leave this hand alone or please don't hit it? You need to be clearer with your words. Last chance, tell me why I'm doing this and you keep the hand."

"I-I don't k-know. Please don't d-do this."

The man shrugged and pulled the crowbar back into a ready position.

"Okay, okay. Wait. Just wait a second. Is this about money? I can get you money. Whatever you want. Just please, don't do th-" He was cut off by a violent whack to his good hand. It flattened like a pancake, sending bits of bone bursting through the skin. Blood leaked from the open wound and ran down the tree trunk.

"Does the name Curtis Hill ring any bells?" the man asked, resting the blood-covered crowbar over his shoulder.

Donny's eyes grew wide with fear. All at once, he knew what was happening and *why* it was happening. But before he could speak, the man swung the bar at Donny's crotch. His pelvis shattered into a million pieces. Donny had never felt pain like this before. Unable to double over, Donny let out a loud scream and blacked out.

"No, no, no, Donny. That is not how this works. You don't get to check out yet." The man pulled a vial of smelling salts from his pocket and stuffed it up Donny's nostril. Donny's eyes bulged as he returned to the land of the conscious.

"P-please d-don't. I-I understand n-now. I-I'm s-sorry."

"What did you do to him you pathetic worm?" The man stared daggers into Donny's eyes. He feared the next words would be his last.

"I-I-I...," he trailed off.

The man pressed the tip of the crowbar under Donny's chin, lifting his head up.

"You want this to end, say what you did to the boy."

Feared welled inside Donny like an overflowing fountain. It burst through his body all at once. Like a bottle popping its cork.

"It started out harmless. Just a few touches here and there. Our little fucking secret. I told him he'd get in trouble if anyone found out. But it's not all my fault. The little tease wanted it just as badly as I did. That's why he came around so often. What was I supposed to do? He was just asking for it. No, begging for it. Coming over like that. Finally, I couldn't help myself. The little touches weren't enough. I had to have the real fucking thing. I shouldn't have done it. I don't know what came over me. I'm sick. I need help. I-I swear to *fucking* god I'll never do it again. Please, just let me live!"

"You raped a child, dirtbag. You don't deserve the air you're breathing now. In fact..."

The man took another powerful swing, aimed at Donny's chest. His ribs snapped like twigs and his chest caved inward. The man watched as Donny struggled to take in gulps of air, but nothing would come. As Donny slowly suffocated, the man merely watched.

Once Donny's body went limp, the man dropped the crowbar and exhaled. The hard part was over. He removed the ax from the tree and began to dismember the body. Each burial spot had been meticulously planned out ahead of time. No one identifying part would be buried near another. Donny would be as good as lost to the world.

Several grueling hours went by before the man returned to his car, Dirt caked his shoes, face, and hands. Nothing a good, hot shower wouldn't fix back home. But first, he had a phone call to make. He punched in the numbers on his phone and waited for the voice on the other end to answer.

"Hello, Ms. Hill. This is detective Thorne. Calling to give you an update on the case of your son's rapist. Unfortunately, his trail has gone *cold.* I'm afraid, no one will ever be able to find him."

"Thank you, detective. I appreciate everything you've done for us."

With that, the pair hung up. Ms. Hill knew exactly what he had meant. The plan had gone off without a hitch. No one would ever be able to find Donny. Of that, he was certain.

Stranger by the Fire

They toasted marshmallows and conversed about old memories. The campfire always brought out these kinds of conversations in the group. One weekend a year was always spent at the same campground with the same people. It made it easier to reminisce about the good old days. The fire popped and crackled between jokes and roars of laughter. The group was happy to be here together.

"I look forward to this trip every year," Amanda said, helping herself to another marshmallow from the bag. She skewered it with the retractable prong and held it over the fire. Within seconds, it burst into flames.

"It's better if you slow roast them. Get that golden-brown look," Brent said as he plucked his marshmallow off the stick. It was the perfect shade of golden brown. As he stuffed it in his mouth, a look of pure satisfaction curled across his face.

"You've been roasting that one for the past ten minutes," Nolan said with a chuckle. "I ain't got the time or patience for that shit." Nolan took his marshmallow and rammed it into the flames. When it caught fire, he pulled it out and blew it out. The force of his breath caused the treat to tumble off the stick and land in the dirt. Everyone laughed.

"That's why I take my time," Brent said, giving him a friendly push.

"You know what, doesn't bother me," Nolan said, reaching down to pick up the marshmallow. "Dirt won't kill you." Before anyone could protest, he shoved it in his mouth and swallowed it down.

"I'd call you disgusting but I don't think it surprised any of us," Tracey said and everyone laughed.

The group of four sat by the flames and talked about life. They talked about what they had been up to this past year. How their lives had changed since the last camping trip. What was better and what was worse. This yearly trip was a way to stay in contact and keep an old tradition alive.

Ever since they were teenagers, the four of them had taken this same camping trip. The same time of year, every year. They had made a pact long ago to always come back. And each year, they kept that promise. No one ever missed a year. Despite marriages and kids and jobs, the four of them kept coming back to this same spot year after year.

All of them had changed since that first trip. Brent had been the jock when they were teens. He was a walking cliché. Played on the football team, drove the red sports car, and even picked on the nerdy kid in math class. Now, he was a middle-aged accountant at a large firm. The sports car got traded for a mini-van many years ago. He no longer played sports and barely watched them anymore. His family had become bigger and more important.

Nolan had been the class clown. Always getting in trouble for cracking jokes when he should be studying. Everyone always thought he would pursue a career in comedy of some kind. It seemed to be his passion. But after his first wife died, so did his comedic tendencies. Now, he would still crack the occasional joke and try to make others laugh but it was different. The same passion wasn't behind it. Nolan had changed the day his wife died.

Tracey loved fashion and makeup in her younger years. Always keeping up with the latest trends, Tracey had been voted best dressed in the yearbook all four years of high school. She had skipped days due to bad hair or make-up. Those who knew her then would hardly recognize her now. Most days, she wore sweatpants and old tee shirts.

Amanda had changed the least. She had always been the sensible one. Not one for wild parties or staying out too late. Everyone thought she would be the perfect person when she was older. The house, the kids, the husband, everything. She would settle and be a housewife and nothing more. Though, these days she still didn't take risks, she was far from her husband and kids. For some reason, she never settled down. Still, she wasn't out into the late hours of the night at clubs and bars meeting men. Instead, she was in bed with a good book by ten almost every night.

A twig snapped nearby and Nolan dropped his marshmallow. "Oh, damnit!" he called out while the others turned to see what had caused the noise.

A man had emerged from the darkness and approached the campfire. His hands were raised like he was surrendering to the group. There was a crooked smile painted across his face. For almost a minute, no one spoke. The man continued to approach the campfire.

"Who the hell are you, pal?" Brent said, a little of his old jock-like voice coming through.

"Someone who just wants to sit and talk, friend," the man said behind his southern drawl.

They all exchanged looks, not sure what to think. Nolan nodded and motioned for the man to sit down. Everyone seemed to relax at this. If Nolan was approving it, then they had nothing to worry about. He had always been the one in charge of these trips which made him sort of the group leader. If he didn't seem worried, then neither did anyone else.

"It's a beautiful night for a campfire," the stranger began as he sat down between Amanda and Tracey. "I went camping by myself, you see, and started to get lonely out there. The woods can be a dark and creepy place, you see. And, well, I could hear you guys laughing and having all sorts of fun and I wanted to join you. I hope I'm not imposing."

"Oh, not at all," Nolan said, pulling his next marshmallow from the fire. "The more the merrier, right guys?" Everyone nodded.

"Forgive me, y'all. Where are my manners?" he said, flashing a smile. "My name is Bert."

"Hey there, Bert," Nolan said with his mouth full. "I'm Nolan. That's Trent. And one either side of you is Tracey and Amanda."

They all smiled and waved but no one said anything. It seemed everyone was waiting on edge for something to happen. Having this stranger by the fire made everyone uneasy.

"Well, y'all seem to be a talkative bunch so I guess I should explain my intentions," Bert said with a smile. "You see, it's been a while since I've had any fun." He chuckled at the last word like he was privy to some inside joke. Nolan chewed his marshmallow and smiled, already preparing a second one. The others shifted in their seats, giving each other worried looks.

"And my idea of fun," the stranger continued. "Is different from others, which is why I don't get to have it all that often. But seeing as we are all out here with no one else around, maybe we ought to have fun together."

"You talking about an orgy or something?" Nolan laughed.

"Not at all, friend," the stranger said as he reached into his pocket and revealed a large knife. "I was thinking more along the lines of a blood bath." The stranger started to laugh maniacally but stopped short when Nolan started to laugh too.

Tracey, Amanda, and Brent all stared at him, wondering what would happen next.

"I'm sorry," Nolan started. "It's just, we started to come on these camping trips years ago because all four of us have something in common. Of course, back then there were five of us. We weren't like anyone else in high school. So, we started to meet in these woods to be who we truly are."

The man with the knife gave a visible yawn and flicked the knife in the air to show his impatience. Nolan kept his cool. The others around the fire tensed and waited for Nolan to finish.

"As the years went on, we kept coming out here to be ourselves until one day it all went wrong. My wife paid the ultimate price. Some asshole stabbed her right through the heart. That's when we stopped playing our little games. That's when we all grew up."

"Oh, so you're all like me," Bert said, smiling.

"Not exactly," Nolan said. He snarled like a wild dog and showed a set of pointed fangs. Waiting for this queue, the others did the same. Each person around the fire brandished a mouth full of razor-sharp teeth except for the stranger.

The grin melted from his face, replaced by absolute terror. The knife slipped from his fingers and he stood up to run. Tracey and Amanda were on him faster than lightning. Two deep bites appeared on his neck. He screamed in excruciating pain and fell to his knees. Both women gripped one of his arms in her hand. His desperate struggles were futile. Brent dashed over and placed two hands on either side of Brent's face. Tears rolled down his cheeks now as he pleaded for his life.

"Buddy," Nolan said as he calmly walked over. "I think you chose the wrong campfire."

With that, the group begin to sink their teeth into his soft flesh and drank his blood until there was nothing left. His dried-up husk was tossed aside like a used napkin. The four of them savored the taste of human blood, which they had not experienced in years. It felt invigorating. It was their first proper meal in ages.

The Captive

It's been days, maybe even weeks since I've been here. I have no concept of time in this dark place. The only way I'm able to judge days passing is by the dinner delivery I receive. It's the only meal a day I get. Otherwise, I sit in this dark room and I cry. There's nothing more I can do.

Try to escape? Well, of course, I've tried that. The first few days, that's all I did. I looked for weak points in the room, tried to pry the door off the hinges, and tried to bang and scream and yell. Nothing happened. The person keeping me here didn't even come to shut me up. Either he likes the sounds of my struggles, or this place is soundproofed.

I came to realize there was no sense in struggling anymore. There was no escape from this place, and no one was ever going to hear me. Besides, my strength started to leave me. All I get a day is a small cup of water and a minimal ration of food. Not enough to satisfy me, but enough to stay alive. After a while, my energy became reduced to almost zero. Even if I wanted to get up and scream, I doubt my body could manage it. I grow weaker by the day.

For the first few days, fear gripped me. Then that fear turned to anger. I hated the person doing this to me. But now, that anger has turned to longing. If only I knew why this was being done to me. I think I've long passed the acceptance stage of grief. Now, I want to know *why?* At least, if the man came in here and tortured me, I would understand he was a psychopath and enjoyed it. Kidnapping someone to let them rot away makes no sense. What purpose does it serve?

And don't think I haven't tried to find out. Most days, when the hooded man brings me my food, I beg and plead to be told why I'm here. In the whole time I've been here, they haven't uttered a single word to me. To be honest, I'm not even sure the person holding me hostage is a man or a woman. I haven't even seen their face. They drop off the food and go. It's almost like they don't want to be in the room with me. What kind of psychopath doesn't enjoy watching their victims get tortured?

In the early days, a chain kept me bound to the wall. But once I became too weak to hardly move, the chains disappeared. They vanished one day while I was sleeping. It's terrifying to think someone was inches from my body while I slept but then again, this whole affair is.

They say Stockholm syndrome can start to materialize in people held captive. A hostage may start to sympathize with their captor or even believe they are there to help after some time. If I ever make it out of this alive, they're going to have to come up with a new syndrome. One where the captive person longs for a relationship with the captive. I'm sure my situation is unique. It may sound bizarre, but I would give anything to know my captor.

I haven't given up yet, in case that was what you were thinking. I still don't want to die. Even after everything I've been through, I still know I need to hang on to hope that I'll make it through this. And because my captor has yet to threaten me or show any hostility, there's a good chance that may happen. If he continues to bring me food and water every day, I can stay alive long enough for rescue to come. There must be someone looking for me. I have friends and family out there. Someone is worried about me. The police are most likely involved. And the longer he keeps me alive, the better chance I have at being found.

Somewhere in the back of my mind, the fear that the food and water will stop coming flutters. It's a thought I would rather keep buried but it keeps fighting its way to the surface. I don't want to starve to death. I'm weak and in enough pain, as it is. I can't imagine more of this. I always thought drowning would be the worst way to go but starvation may have it beat. I have no energy and can barely move but I feel every ounce of pain from my body starving to death. Only, I never quite get there because of the small portions keeping me alive. It's excruciating. And like I said, the will to live is still present. I would have thought death would be an embrace in a situation like this, but it isn't.

There's still so much I haven't done. So much I want to see. Things I want to do. I always put off traveling because I figured there would be time later. Being locked in this room is giving me too much time to think. If my captor was in here torturing me every day, I would be begging for death. But the loneliness and silence only serve to make me long for the life I *could* be living. And maybe that's what my captor is doing to me. Maybe he knows this is the worst torture of all. Leaving me alone with my thoughts while I slowly starve to death. Only, what pleasure does it bring him? I still don't understand.

I've looked around the room for cameras or peepholes. I thought, maybe he watches my misery from the safety of another room. There seems to be nothing. If he is watching me, I have no idea how. Still, if my captor was watching me, I don't understand what pleasure it brings. This must be the most boring torture to watch. I spend most of my days sitting here, doing nothing.

If you want the story about how I was captured, I'm sorry to disappoint. I don't remember. Everything before this room is blurry. Thinking about it now, most of my life before this room is a blur. Was I married? Did I have kids? Where did I work? How old was I? What is my name? I...I can't remember. No matter how hard I try, I can't remember any of it. It seems all I can remember now is this damned room.

It must be the starvation and the delirium getting to me. How could someone forget all those things about themselves? Could it be possible that I have amnesia? I have no idea how to tell if that's what I have. There's always the possibility my captor drugged me to keep me from remembering. Maybe it's in the food. But I don't know if a drug like that exists. I want to remember something about my life. Anything. I want to more than I want freedom from this place. If I could at least remember what I have at home, maybe I would remember what's worth fighting for. I could remember why I want to make it out of here alive.

Refusing to eat would only get me killed. At this point, I feel missing even one meal would make me pass out and die. And I've come too far to die like that now. I'm not going to give the bastard in the other room the satisfaction. After all this time, I've concluded that watching a person slowly die brings them joy. He doesn't like torture or gore. He likes to watch the life drain from another human being. Well, I'm not going to give him the satisfaction. Next time he comes in here, I'm going to use the last bit of my strength to attack him and knock him to the floor. Even if I don't manage to escape, I would like to at least see his face. Ask him why. Tonight, I will get answers...

Last night, I managed to spring on my captor while he was bringing me food. The events which transpired after are hard to explain. First, I should explain that my captor has always dressed in baggy, black clothing. A hoodie and baggy pants. Black gloves. Everything covered. I've never so much as seen a small patch of skin. So, yesterday when I leaped through the air and rammed my body into his, I was surprised when nothing happened. I found myself on the floor in a mess of black clothing. Thinking my captor had somehow thrown off his clothes, I managed to look up from the floor in my weakened state. There was nothing there. All that was left was a pile of clothing. There was no possible way he had escaped as I had landed closer to the door. But somehow, he had vanished.

As unbelievable as it sounds, no one has been bringing me food this entire time. And yet, someone had been bringing me food. My mind raced with questions when as I lay sprawled out on the floor in my weak state. I started to wonder how much of it all was an illusion. If the person bringing me food wasn't real, what else wasn't real? Which brought me to a more important question. If the food wasn't real, how was I still alive? Why was I weak? That's when I realized I wasn't weak anymore. The feelings of starvation and hunger were gone.

I pulled myself to my feet and looked around. Was the room an illusion, too? But it didn't disappear like the captor or my symptoms. The first thing I did was try the door and found it locked. Whatever was going on, I was truly trapped in this room. If I was trapped, why the illusions? More importantly, how? That's when I heard, felt, and smelled everything around me. There were screams in the distance. Howling screams of pain and immense suffering. The air around me was stifling and hot. And last, I smelled the brimstone. That was the giveaway.

My knees buckled and I collapsed on the floor. This whole time I had wondered why my captors hadn't told me why I was here and why they were doing this to me. I spent so much time sitting in that corner feeling weak and hungry, wondering when I would starve to death. The answer was clear now. I was already dead and in hell. This room, this torture, was hell. At least, my hell.

Like a dull headache, I could feel these current memories start to fade away. Like the memories of who I was before this, I wouldn't remember a thing. Desperate to remember, I found something to write with and some old slips of paper and I wrote down my story. I placed the paper on top of an old desk in the corner of the dilapidated room. I noticed an open drawer and hundreds upon thousands of handwritten notes inside. Sifting through them as fast as I could, I realized they all had one thing in common. I had written them. All outlining my story, trapped in hell. How long have I been here? I tried to cry but tears wouldn't form. Instead, the memories started to drift away faster.

Now, the chain has wrapped around my ankle again and I'm having trouble remembering even more. Soon, I fear I will be back in that corner and starving all over again. I didn't want to die before. I wanted to survive so I could escape. Now, I want to die for good. I wish the afterlife was nothing but darkness instead of this terrible...

It's been days, maybe even weeks since I've been here...

The Man Dressed as Santa

"It looks like we have another gift for you, Miranda," the jolly-sounding man dressed as Santa said. "Go ahead, open it up. I'm sure we're all dying to know what's inside."

"Go to hell," Miranda said, pulling against her restraints.

"Now, now, Miranda. That is *naughty* behavior. You were on the nice list this year. Don't make me change my mind," he said with a raspy laugh. "Besides, it's from Tom! Don't you want to know what he gave you this year?"

"Leave her alone!" Tom yelled from across the room, pulling against the ropes that bound him.

"Fine, I guess this gift is out," the Santa said as he kicked the present across the room like a soccer ball.

Miranda, Tom, and five other guests sat around a well-lit Christmas tree. Ropes wrapped around each person like little human presents. Only the man dressed as Santa could move about. He bounced here and there like a jolly elf, handing out presents that no one could open.

"What the hell do you want with us?" a black-haired woman screamed.

The Santa turned to her, giving a hearty laugh.

"Why, Laurie, I'm here to give presents to the nice and to punish the naughty. Which list do you think you're on this year, hmm?" He laughed as he pulled a list from his pocket.

"Please," Tom said. "Take whatever you want. We have money if you want that. Just leave us all alone."

The Santa smirked and stuffed the list back in his pocket. He turned towards Tom with a flourish of his hands.

"Tsk, tsk, Tommy. That sounds like a bribe. Are you trying to bribe Santa Claus? That is most naughty. But I suppose I should expect nothing less from you. *You* are already on the naughty list. Isn't that right, Laurie?"

Laurie and Tom locked eyes for a moment. Miranda looked back and forth at the two of them. Santa turned to face Laurie and pulled the list back from his pocket.

"Ahem, Laurie and Tom. Both were *very* naughty this year. They were naughty in the hotel room, naughty in the hot tub, and my goodness! Naughty in Tom and Miranda's own bed! That's very naughty. Tsk, tsk."

Miranda scowled at the two of them. Her face begged for answers. Neither Tom nor Laurie spoke up. Miranda hung her head in disappointment and resentment.

"Yes, yes. Poor Miranda. Now, moving on!" Santa snapped his head towards the other guests in the room. "Ah, yes. Let's see. We have covered Miranda, Tom, and Laurie. Nice, naughty, and naughty. Who is next? Oh! Matt and Linda. Were you naughty or nice this year?"

"Let us go you crazy sonofabitch!" Matt yelled, pulling on his restraints.

The Santa approached Matt's seat. He bent down low and looked Matt in the eyes. Without looking down at his list, he said, "Naughty."

"You're just some lunatic who drugged us all and tied us up! There's nothing about us you could possibly know," Matt said.

Santa arced his arm across the room, pointer finger extended. It landed on a blonde-haired woman crying to herself.

"Jennifer and Matt. Oh, *very* naughty this year."

He approached Jennifer and gave her a little pat on the belly.

"Naughty indeed!"

Matt lifted his head and looked straight at Jennifer. His wife, Linda, looked over at him. Tears flooded her eyes.

"Jennifer, you're pregnant?" Matt asked.

She nodded.

"I mean, that's great news. Uh, who is the father? I didn't even know you were-"

"Oh, shut the fuck up, Matt," Linda said. "I know you've been fucking her. It's your fucking baby, you piece of shit."

"Sweetheart, I-"

"Don't you sweetheart, me. I've been suspecting it for months. Just never had the proof."

"You can't possibly believe this crazy man in a Santa suit, can you?"

The Santa Claus reeled back in mock offense. Then he gave a little chuckle and skipped about the room. He stopped in front of Jonathan and collapsed on his lap. No one said a word.

"What about you, Jonathan? Have you been naughty?"

Jonathan stared at the Santa in his lap, staying quiet.

"Let's see, let's do a quick recap, shall we? Ahem. Tom has been naughty with Miranda's best friend, Laurie. Miranda, of course, is nice. Matt has been naughty with Linda's friend, Jennifer. Linda has also been nice. I see a pattern forming here, don't you?" Santa let out a cheerful laugh. "The married women are all nice while all the married men are naughty. The single women are all naughty. But what about the single man? Naughty or nice?"

Jonathan looked up into Santa's face, staring daggers.

"I'm not playing your fucking games," he said in a low, gruff voice.

Santa clapped and dismounted the man.

"Yes, there is an idea! Games! I have the perfect one. But we need to divide into groups. How about naughty versus nice?"

The Santa walked over to Tom and grabbed the ropes wrapped around his body. He dragged him across the room and flung him to the floor. He did the same with Matt, Jennifer, and Laurie. Only Miranda, Linda, and Jonathan remained in their seats.

"Alright, Jonathan. Here are the rules. I'm going to ask you four questions, one for each *naughty* person here. If you get them all right, you get a big prize! But for each one you get wrong, I take one away."

Jonathan shook his head and closed his eyes. "I don't care what you're fucking prizes are. I'm not playing."

"First question, Johnny. Were you naughty or nice this year?" Santa asked with a laugh.

"I'm not answering your fucking questions. Go ahead and take a *prize* away. I don't want them, anyway," Jonathan said.

The Santa gave an exaggerated frown.

"I think these gifts you will want to keep, Johnny boy. I'll give you one more chance. Were you naughty or nice this year?"

"Fuck you!"

"Sorry, that answer is incorrect. You have lost one prize!"

Before Jonathan could say another word, the Santa leaped across the room. He wrapped his fingers around Matt's throat and squeezed. Matt choked and sputtered as everyone in the room begged the Santa to stop. Matt struggled under the large man. His eyes bulged and his skin turned blue. Both Linda and Jennifer screamed for it to stop.

"I'll play your fucking games! Just stop!" Jonathan yelled. But it was too late. Matt's body went limp. Tears cascaded down Linda's cheeks as she stared at her husband's swollen face.

"Only...three...prizes...left," the Santa panted as he stood up.

"You're a fucking psychopath!" Jonathan screamed. "What have you done?"

"Ha! Not me, you naughty boy. *You* did this, Jonathan. I told you the rules. You refused to answer the question. Besides, Matt was naughty. He needed to be punished. But don't worry anymore, Jonathan. We have three more questions to answer and you have three more prizes to win...or lose."

The Santa broke into a burst of strange laughter that sounded jolly and maniacal. It sent shivers down everyone's spines. Linda shook with fear, tears still streaming down her face. She had yet to look away from her husband's lifeless body.

Jennifer whimpered to herself. So much had happened in the past few minutes and her head was a whirlwind of thoughts. She dared quick glances at Matt's body, trying her best to avoid Linda.

Jonathan and Miranda sat in silence, staring down at the scene before them. Their friend's body lay in the middle of the room like a heap of laundry. On the floor around him, Tom, Laurie, and Jennifer wiggled against their bindings. The whole picture was surreal. The dancing Santa Claus in the middle of it all brought it to a whole new level.

"All right, Johnny boy. Question number two. Did you enjoy being naughty this year?"

Jonathan scrunched up his face.

"What?"

"Fair enough, Johnny boy. I'll give you one more chance to answer the question since it was a little unfairly worded. Try it this way, did you have fun being naughty with *her?*"

Jonathan shook his head. "I don't underst-" His eyes grew wide like a memory struck him. The Santa grinned from ear to ear as he nodded.

"Oh yes, Johnny boy. You understand the question now. I can see it in your face. Now, answer the question. And before you do, know the answer must be the truth or you lose another prize. Santa always knows when you're lying," the Santa said the last few words with a sing-song voice and twisted smile.

Jonathan hung his head low.

"Yes," he whispered.

"Yes, you enjoyed being naughty with her? Is that what you're saying, Johnny boy?"

"Yes! I enjoyed every fucking second of it. Is that what you wanted to hear you twisted, evil fuck?" Jonathan snapped.

Miranda looked over at Jonathan. The two locked eyes for a moment before he hung his head in shame.

"Jonathan, what is he talking about? What happened? What did you do?"

"No!" the Santa screamed. "Don't ruin the game! We're so close to the end now. And look, Johnny, you get a prize. Now, which one to pick?"

"Let Jennifer go," Jonathan said without hesitation. "She's pregnant. You have to let her go."

The man dressed as Santa let out the loudest laugh yet. He doubled over, clutching at his sides. Wiping tears from his eyes, he looked at Jonathan.

"That's a good one, Johnny boy. But very well. Your prize is Jennifer!" He pulled Jennifer up by her ropes and tossed her on the couch next to Miranda. She rolled over and sat upright.

"Two more questions and two more prizes. Will Jonathan take them both home?" The Santa said in the tone of a game show host. "This is all so very fun, isn't it?"

Jonathan said nothing. He stared at the Santa, ready for the next question.

"Third question, Johnny boy. What did you do with the body?"

Miranda's eyes grew wide with fear as her head turned towards her friend. Jennifer shook in her seat, inching closer to Miranda for safety. Linda was still tied to her chair a few feet from the Christmas tree. She looked down at the body of Matt and the figures of Tom and Laurie. They had stopped moving now, both necks craned to look up at Jonathan.

"I...I...uh," Jonathan stammered. "I hid it in a dumpster." Tears fell from his eyes.

"Hmm, while technically your answer is correct, that's not the full answer Jonathan," Santa said, wagging his finger. He stepped over the bodies on the floor and approached the unlit fireplace. He grabbed a fire poker from the mantle and walked over between Tom and Laurie.

"Please, don't. I'll go on. I'll say it all. You didn't give me the chance to finish," Jonathan pleaded.

The Santa stared at Jonathan for a moment, his eyes flicking back and forth to the fire poker. Thoughts seemed to be racing through his head. Jonathan only stared.

"Sorry, time's up Johnny boy." The Santa raised the fire poker above his head and brought it down with tremendous force on Tom's skull. The poker pierced through his forehead and stuck into the floor below, killing Tom. Blood oozed from his wounds as his eyes fluttered several times before stopping in a blank stare.

"Oh God!" Jonathan cried out. "Why did you do that? I answered your question."

"Gotta get your answer in before the buzzer, Johnny boy," the Santa said with a laugh.

He bent over and grabbed the ropes around Laurie and hoisted her into the air. She dangled like a perverted Christmas ornament before the Santa placed her in a chair near the fireplace. He turned back towards the crowd and stared at Jonathan.

"Ready for the final round, Jonathan?"

Jonathan swallowed hard.

"Oh, aren't these Christmas games always just so exciting?" the Santa said. "All right, all right. Final question. Here it is. What was her name."

Jonathan stared at the Santa for a moment. The white-bearded man swung his finger in the air to imitate a clock ticking away. The silence in the room was deafening. He swallowed again. A short breath escaped his lips.

"S-sil-"

"Yes, come on, Johnny boy. You can do it. Say the name of the woman you raped and murdered. The same woman whose throat you cut and chopped up into little pieces and tossed in the dumpster like fucking trash. SAY HER

FUCKING NAME!" The Santa dropped his silly demeanor now. Anger screamed out of every pore.

"S-Silvia M-Moore," Jonathan whimpered.

"That's right! Mrs. *Fucking* Claus!" Santa screamed. He pulled a revolver from his waistband and fired two bullets into Jonathan's chest. As the man choked for air, the Santa drew closer. He pressed the barrel against Jonathan's head.

"Her name will be the last words out of your pathetic mouth you piece of human garbage. See you in hell."

The Santa pulled the trigger.

Jonathan's body went limp. Only the ropes held him in place. Not a single person moved or said a word. The smell of gun powder hung heavy in the air. The Santa stood there, staring at Jonathan's body, looking relieved.

"It's finally over," he said at last. "The man who raped you and the two that helped are dead. You can rest now, my love," he whispered.

The group exchanged worried glances. There was no telling if the torment from this man dressed as Santa was over or not. Learning their friend Jonathan had raped and murdered a woman would not be an easy truth to swallow. Even worse, knowing Matt and Tom were involved would drive them mad. Nothing any one of them could say in this moment would help or make sense. So, everyone remained silent. They waited for whatever fate the Santa would bring upon them.

"I'm sorry," the Santa sniffled. "The rest of you are free to go. The police will be here shortly to release you. Goodbye."

The Santa turned and headed for the door. The crazed movements and bizarre jolly nature had left his body. He now seemed only to be the shell of a broken man. Revenge was his, but it did not bring him peace. That much was obvious to everyone.

"Uh, Santa?" Jennifer said. He turned to face her. "I'm sorry about your wife." She let her words linger in the air like snowflakes.

"Me too," he said, turning back towards the door. He stopped and glanced back at her over his shoulder. "Maybe not so naughty after all," he said as he slipped out the front door.

Still tied up, the survivors looked at each other. All made sure to avoid looking at the bodies around them. Before they could say a word about escape, they heard a loud *bang!* in the front yard. There was a loud thudding sound and the crunching of snow before utter silence. They all knew what had happened, but no one wanted to say it. It was best to sit and wait for the police to come and rescue them. The man dressed as Santa was gone.

Drag it to Hell

All around me, there was only darkness. I couldn't move, I couldn't speak, and I couldn't see. But I could smell something. There was a pungent odor in the air like a bag of pennies in a pot of potting soil. It was a putrid smell that made me want to vomit. I could almost feel the bile rise in my throat. So, I wasn't dead. At least, not yet.

The feeling started to return to my limbs. I moved my right hand, careful not to move too fast. My nails dug into the soft earth below. The dirt was wet and fowl. Fear flowed through my veins. A pain in my right shoulder erupted like a long-dormant volcano. My eyes snapped open and I found myself staring at the ground below. Sitting up to nurse my shoulder, I spotted a heap only a few feet away.

It was dusk in the middle of the woods and my eyes had yet to adjust. Minutes passed before I finally realized what I was looking at. There was a human body slumped over in the middle of the small clearing around me. Judging by the crimson-soaked dirt below, I figured the person was dead.

I crawled towards the body with caution. I had a feeling deep in my gut that I would regret what I found. When I rolled the body on its back, I cried. I cried like I never had before. Staring back at me, with lifeless eyes, was the body of my wife. Her flowing red hair matted against her pale skin, a tangled mess. With a single finger, I brushed the hair out of her face. Her lifeless eyes stared back at me with a glazing stare. I cried and shook her but she never moved.

When I had accepted the inevitable and moved away from her body, I noticed the blood on my hands. Why was her blood on my hands? Why was she dead? I racked my brain for any memory of the previous night's events, but nothing came. It felt like looking through a thick fog. The memories were there but too hazy to recall.

The pain erupted in my shoulder again. Pulling down the collar of my shirt, I spotted a wound. Dry blood circled the wound and a small drizzle of fresh blood still seemed to ooze out. Lightly pressing the tip of my finger against it caused white-hot pain. My eyes scanned the forest floor for any sign of a weapon. Whatever had caused this wound had to be nearby.

I spotted it but not where I ever would have suspected it. Clutched in my wife's rigor mortis-ridden clutch was a handgun. There was doubt it had been the weapon to create my wound.

Out of nowhere, a memory struck me like a woodland creature in the path of a semi-truck. Part of the fog in my mind lifted and I saw Savannah's face, clear as day. I wished I could stay there forever, at that moment. But it quickly turned dark. I could see a gun in her hand but the thought of her was still blurry. I couldn't make out where she had been when it was pointed at me. All I could remember was the gun her the words she used. "No, don't." Then, it fired. That's all that flooded back.

What the hell had happened? Why had Savanah shot me? And did I hurt her? Now, I had to do the unthinkable and search her body for clues. Other than a slit throat, which nearly made me hysterical, I found nothing.

Unsure of what to do next, I pried the gun from her hands and thought. It seemed best to find help but I didn't want to just leave her. Having no tools to bury her with, I decided to head out in search of help. I tried to swat away the thought of wolves or vultures happening upon her body.

The woods were dark and quiet. Every few minutes, I glanced over my shoulder. A feeling of being watched kept falling over me. There was something out there, I was sure of it. But it was the forest. Of course, there was something out there. Birds, owls, snakes, bears, wolves. What wasn't out there?

I heard a twig snap in the distance and my heart stopped. All sorts of vicious creatures ran through my mind. Every one of them could maul me to death in the blink of an eye. I was not prepared for what found me.

"Alan?" a soft voice called from behind a tree. It couldn't be. It wasn't possible. Savannah stepped out and looked at me with those big, beautiful eyes and I almost wept with relief. I forgot about the slit throat and the body. I even forgot the pain in my shoulder. My thoughts were only of her.

Instinctively, I ran to her. I threw my arms around her and cried. The gun fell and half-buried in the dirt below. She said something soft in my ear, but I couldn't quite make it out. "What, sweetheart?" I asked, pulling away. She looked straight into my eyes. Those beautiful hazel eyes I remembered were not there. I almost tripped over my own feet. In their place stood two burning embers. In another moment, they were gone. Her hazel eyes were back and she looked at me longingly.

"What's the matter?" she asked. I didn't know what to do or say. Had it been my imagination? It must have been. My nerves were shot and I was lost in a creepy forest. But the image of the lifeless body of my beloved wife came flooding back. I looked down at my blood-stained hands. It couldn't have been my imagination. Whatever this thing was, it wasn't my wife. Every fiber of my being told me to run. Something else told me it was already too late.

The thing stared at me with hopeful eyes. It seemed to be waiting for my next move. There was a brief moment, a fraction of a second, where her eyes flicked to my hand then back at my eyes. I would have missed it had I not been staring. Now, the thing imitating my wife seemed nervous. I was nervous too.

My wife's hands touched my arm and I had to fight back the feeling of comfort and affection. I knew it wasn't her. Her silky-smooth hands slid down my arm, heading for my hand. For the gun!

My feet moved before I could think. My arm pulled up into the air at the same time. They seemed to move separate from me, almost with a mind of their own. I stood, arm outstretched, and a gun in my wife's tear-filled face.

"Please," She pleaded. I shook my head. Whatever this thing was, I couldn't let it leave. It cried and there was a fleeting moment of doubt before my finger squeezed the trigger.

The bullet ripped through her forehead and a mixture of pain and betrayal spread across her face. I immediately regretted everything and dropped to her side. It was too late. She was gone before she hit the ground. Her body felt cold to the touch. I picked up her hand and pressed it against my face and cried.

"I'm so sorry. What have I done?" I cried harder than I thought possible. Had I killed my wife? What had come over me? I remembered the body I had woken up next to. That had been Savannah, I was sure of it. Was I going crazy? I hoped so.

My mind wouldn't rest until I had proof. Pushing away from my wife's body, for the second time that day, I ran through the woods until I found it. With apprehension, I approached the slumped-over body. It was her. How could this be? Was I seeing things? That had to be the answer.

When I turned away to hide from the sight, I was greeted with a twisted smile. It was my wife again. The bullet hole still stood in her forehead like a haunting reminder of what I had done.

Then, a memory flooded back so violently, I almost fell backward. A campfire burned between the two of us. The smoke rose overhead to a peaceful night sky. My wife smiled at me and ate the s'more in her hands. Melted chocolate and marshmallow smeared against her cheek. She looked at me and smiled. I loved her non-apologetic ways. At that moment, I found her the most beautiful woman on the planet and I fell in love all over again.

It was interrupted by something darting through the trees. We both jumped but I tried to play it tough. "Don't worry, it was probably just a raccoon." I knew it had sounded much bigger and I could tell she could see through my charade. Through the flames, I peered into the dark forest and I caught something looking back. When it stepped from the tree line, we both gasped and jumped to our feet.

Now, I was staring at the thing which had stepped into our campsite. That seemed like weeks ago. Somehow, it had transformed from my wife and back to its true, disgusting form. I didn't even see it happen. This thing stared at me with blood-thirsty eyes. Its tall, slender frame hunched over and yet still towered over me. The dark, leathery skin which covered its body reminded me of something ripped from a nightmare. Long, animal-like talons stretched from its fingers. Razor-sharp teeth barred out at me from behind a wicked grin.

With a shaky hand, I raised the pistol. The creature sneered in what I assumed was laughter. It was at that moment I knew my gun would do nothing to stop it. Regardless, I had to try. A reptilian-like tongue emerged from its mouth and a string of drool hung from its lips. It was hungry.

I squeezed the trigger and the round caught the creature in the shoulder. It hissed and vanished before my eyes. There was no reason to wait around for its return so I ran as fast as I could. I ran until my lungs burned and my legs collapsed. Strewn about beneath a tree, I caught my breath.

As I did, another memory came back. My wife and I had run from the creature in our camp. We had run until we couldn't go on. When we collapsed, it had been in a bog. The water came up to our knees. Normally, I'd worry about snakes or alligators, but my mind had only been focused on what had chased us. That had been when Savannah found the bodies. Hundreds of them. They floated in the bog-like pebbles. My first instinct was to run some more but the curious nature of my wife kept us there longer. Which is how we found the gun.

The memory began to fade and reality struck me with a powerful right hook. I looked up at the tree I sat beneath and took deep breaths. The cramp in my side began to subside. When it was gone, I would run some more. Of course, I didn't get the chance to.

A familiar hand reached around the tree and dug its nails into the bark. I yelled and leaped to my feet. Before I could move, the creature was in front of me. It was clear I could no longer run. It would find me wherever I went. My only chance would be to stay and fight.

Drool still dripped from its snarling mouth and rotted flesh rested beneath its nails. I noticed the blood-stained teeth and thought about the bodies in the bog. Then I thought of my wife. She had died because of this...thing. I would send it back to hell.

With a loud yell, I raised the gun and emptied the magazine. Each shot sent the creature back a few inches at a time until it collapsed on the forest floor. There it lay, motionless. Had I won? Was it dead? I should have known better.

It climbed to its feet and the bullet holes seemed to heal before my eyes. This was it. This was how I died. It had taken my wife and now it would take me. There was nothing left to do. As I sunk to my knees to accept my fate, another memory melted through the fog.

My wife and I had made it away from the bog in time to avoid the creature. It didn't take long for it to pick up our trail. When it lunged out of the trees and tackled Savannah, it had looked like me. I couldn't believe my eyes. This thing could look like us. How was it possible? It couldn't be real. But it was all too real.

She had screamed and tried to push the creature off but it was too strong. I jumped on its back but it swatted me away like a fly. Once again, I lunged on the creature and tried to wrestle it away. I saw the fear in Savannah's eyes and the gun in her hands. That's when she said something. "No, don't." I was confused. I didn't know what she meant. But then I saw it. The creature had forced her hand in the air and pointed the gun up at me. Then, it pulled the trigger. Before I blacked out, I watched the terrible thing cut her throat and lap up her blood. It looked at me and winked as I fell into oblivion.

The creature had forced her to shoot me and then slit her throat. But why leave me alive? Unless it liked to hunt. Perhaps it needed to hunt. Either way, it gave me an idea and my only chance.

"Hunt me," I said as the thing stood over me. I could see its hand poised, ready to strike. But it reared back in understanding. It cocked its head and looked at me as if to tell me to go on.

"Let me leave here now and you hunt me."

The reptilian eyes flicked back and forth for a moment, weighing its options. Then, it gave me a sort of nod. "Three days," it sneered and flung itself into the trees. There was a fleeting moment of relief but was soon replaced by terror. There was limited time to get ready.

I'm sitting here writing this by candlelight in an old wooden shack. The three days are about up. I'm not going to run or hide. I don't know what can kill this thing but I'm willing to bet the explosives I've rigged will do the trick. This fucker is going down tonight. I will drag it to hell.

The Surprise

She knew the rules. Don't go into the basement, no matter what. But she was tired of her father treating her like a little girl. She was sixteen now. Almost a woman. Whatever he had down there to hide, she was sure she had seen worse.

Her dad was single and always brought new women by the house. Megan was sure her father was into the weird crap. She pictured a whole dungeon beneath the house complete with sex swings and the works. It was weird to think about her father having sex, but she knew it was a fact of life. It was how every single person on the planet came to be. And her curiosity was too much to bear. She needed to know what was down there.

While her father was out at work, Megan snuck to the basement door. Of course, it was locked. She had expected that. Lucky for her, it was no more than a simple doorknob lock. A rather old one at that. It could be picked with a paperclip given the right amount of patience.

It only took her a few minutes before the lock turned and the knob twisted. Whatever her father was hiding must not have been worth a few extra bucks for a better lock. In Megan's young, teenage mind she convinced herself this was her father's fault. He created curiosity in her by sectioning off part of the house and not locking it down properly.

The door swung open with a creak. Megan stared down at the steps shrouded in darkness. Her hand felt around on the wall for the light switch. Flicking it up did nothing. Either the bulb was burnt out or her father never installed one on purpose.

"Ugh, gross," she said to no one. "Maybe it really is his sex dungeon."

Despite the possibility of seeing her father's sex toys, she descended the steps with caution. It was almost impossible to see in the darkened basement. There were no windows down here and the only light filtered in from the hallway above. It only lit up the top half of the stairs.

As Megan's bare feet slapped against the cold, concrete floor, something moved to her left. She squinted in the darkness, hoping to catch a glimpse. It was like staring at black sheets. Impossible to see through.

"I really hope that wasn't a rat," she said.

With an outstretched hand, Megan crept along the wall. She hoped to find anything that would shed light on the room. Her father really couldn't have used this room in the pitch black, could he? Then her mind went to photography. What if this was a darkroom for photos? If she turned on a light, it could destroy them. She wasn't entirely sure how a darkroom worked. In the movies, they were always lit with a red light. Besides, why would keeping her out of a room full of photos be important? Unless they were nude photos of his lady friends. Megan rolled her eyes at her perverted thoughts.

Her knee bumped something in front of her. Megan stopped and stretched out her hands in the darkness. Again, something moved in the distance. It sounded bigger than a rat. Her heart began to jackhammer in her chest. The thought of turning and running for the stairs fluttered in her mind like a panicked bird. Then her hand grasped something cold and metallic. It took her brain a moment to realize she was holding a candlestick. Light! If only she could find a lighter.

Megan's free hand searched the end table she had bumped into. There had to be a lighter nearby. At least, she hoped. Finally, her hand bumped a small cardboard box. Picking it up, she shook it next to her ear. Matches!

Placing the candlestick down, Megan slid open the box. She struck a match on the side and a small pinprick of light burst forth through the darkness. She craned her neck to look around the basement but could still see nothing. The match was only bright enough to engulf the small area around her in light.

She pressed the match against the candlewick and the light source doubled. It was brighter now, but she still couldn't see far. Another noise broke out to her left. With apprehension, Megan turned towards it and began to walk. As her feet slapped against the concrete floor, the movement ahead of her increased. Something shifted wildly in the dark. A metallic rattle clanged in the small space.

The candlelight illuminated a dark spot in the corner of the room. Megan almost dropped it from her hand when she saw what it had revealed. A woman in tattered clothing, covered in dirt and dried patches of blood. Her arms were constricted by chains that reached up the ceiling. She rested on her shins. Her matted hair was strewn about her head like a bird's nest. Megan could almost make out the woman's face. Over the woman's mouth was a single strip of duct tape.

The woman saw Megan and began to weep. She pulled at the chains, pleading with Megan to set her free. Megan was unable to move. The scene before her was unexpected. She didn't know what to do. The chains rattled as the woman pulled at them with all her might, crying a muffled cry under the tape. Her eyes flicked back and forth from Megan to some unseen entity behind her. Megan's blood ran cold.

"You shouldn't be down here," a familiar voice called out from behind. "You weren't supposed to see this now."

Megan could hear her father's footfalls on the concrete floor now. He was only a few feet behind her. She was unsure of what to do. Should she turn to face him or run for the door? She was worried about what sort of trouble she would be in.

"Well, I suppose the surprise is ruined now," her father said. Tears rolled down the woman's cheeks as he approached behind Megan. She pulled at the chains harder now.

Megan stared at the woman and the two locked eyes. She saw the woman motion towards the door with her head, telling her to run. But Megan still could not move. Her body was not responding to any commands.

"Dad," she said with a tremble in her voice. "What is this?"

Her father let out a laugh.

"It's yours, Megan. You're old enough now. I was saving this as a surprise for you. You've grown into a fine young woman and I think you're ready."

"Ready?" Megan asked, watching the woman's eyes. She still pleaded with Megan to run for her life. Tears rolled down Megan's cheeks now.

"Yes, sweetheart. This was meant to be a surprise for you. It wasn't ready yet. But I suppose now is as good a time as any. Finally, we can share in Daddy's hobby together."

"Your hobby is torture and murder?" Megan asked, turning to face her father for the first time.

"Those are such ugly words, sweetheart. Other people don't understand my hobby and they are forced to label it in terrible ways. But there's nothing wrong with it. The urges are natural. Trust me. Your father has been doing this since before you were born. And now, I want to share it with you."

"Share it with me?" Megan's voice trailed off.

Megan stared at her father with tears in her eyes. She didn't know what to say. She dared a glance back over her shoulder at the woman bound and gagged. Fear gripped the woman's face, but she seemed unable to move any longer. Exhaustion was settling in. There was no telling how long this woman had been down here.

"Dad," she said, looking back at him. "It's perfect!" She jumped forward and wrapped her arms around her father.

After a long embrace, she turned back toward the chained woman. There seemed to be a newfound fear in the captive woman's eyes. She pulled against the chains as she tried to cry out for help. Her muffled screams made Megan laugh.

"Hush, now," Megan said, approaching. Her dad stepped forward and placed a hand on her shoulder. "It's time we have our fun."

Door-to-Door

It was late in the afternoon when the knock came at the door. Visitors weren't something Cassie expected, especially not unannounced like this. But Cassie pulled herself up off the couch and headed towards the door. She had to admit, she was curious who was there. Her mind conjured up images of door-to-door salesmen and pushy religious nut jobs. Neither of which she wanted anything to do with. She would tell them to kindly get lost. It was her time to relax and watch television.

When Cassie pulled open the door, she was greeted by a young man wearing a white shirt and black tie. Religious nut job, no doubt. She couldn't help but wonder how many people this tactic worked on. Did these people believe these surprise sermons converted people to their religion? People either slammed the door in their face or pretended to not be home. The nicer people, like Cassie, would listen to whatever they had to say and then throw the literature in the trash. There couldn't have ever been a person alive who converted to a new religion from a doorway visit.

"Can I help you?" Cassie asked.

"Ma'am, I was wondering if maybe I could help you. Have you heard the good word?" The cheery man announced.

Cassie meant to tell the man to screw off and slam the door in her face. Now, staring him in the face she realized she couldn't do it. The man seemed nice, even if he was preaching about something she had no interest in. Instead, she would politely hear him out and then throw the literature away. No harm.

"Well, I have, as a matter of fact," Cassie said with a cheery voice. "My parents were Catholic, so I know all about it."

"Oh, well that's good to hear. But do you know the full story?"

And there it was. Cassie hated this about these people. Even if you told them you agreed with them, they still found a way to keep talking to you. It was ridiculous. She remembered a time in her youth while working as a cashier. Something similar had happened. On her lunch break, she found herself sitting at the little café in the retail store. An elderly man walked up to her and said hi. Being the polite person she was, she said hi back and smiled. The man then proceeded to ask her if she believed in Jesus Christ. She said yes, which wasn't a complete lie. Cassie wasn't religious, especially not as a teenager, but she didn't outright not believe. But to keep the man from lecturing her, she had told him yes. To her horror, the man took up her entire lunch break talking about the wonders of Jesus and God.

"I think I've heard the stories before. I used to go to church every Sunday with my grandparents," she said to the man now.

"Ah, used to. So, you've fallen out of touch with the almighty?"

She knew she had made a huge mistake. She wanted to slam the door in his face and be done with the encounter, but she couldn't. Cassie hated being mean, even when someone deserved it. Confrontations were not her strongest skills.

"I suppose you could say that. But I still believe in it all. Unfortunately, I might be a waste of your time."

"Nonsense," the man said. "I want to make sure you get into heaven. Some would have you believe that just accepting Jesus into your life will get you into heaven. It's not so simple. I have this brochure here. Would you allow me to read some scripture to you?"

Before Cassie could answer, her cell phone began to ring in the other room. Like an intervention from God, she had a way out. She wasn't going to waste this chance. Cassie made a motion with her head, showing the man at the door she was about to walk away.

"Excuse me, I really need to take this call. It's important."

The man nodded but handed the pamphlet in his hand over. Cassie took it without a second thought. It would end up in the trash, anyway. She smiled as she started to shut the door. The man said something about following up with her later, but she didn't quite hear it. Next time, she would pretend to not be home or in the shower. She wouldn't open up again.

When the door was shut, she raced to the other room and picked up her phone. The screen said *scam likely*. She laughed at the coincidence and tossed the phone on the end table. How many unsolicited attempts could happen at once?

Taking the pamphlet, the man had given her, Cassie made her way to the trash can. She tossed it in without giving it a second thought. Her conversation with the man was over and she'd never have to endure it again.

A couple of days went by and the man never came back. Every day, she expected a knock at the door, but it never came. It seemed the man had forgotten all about her. After work later in the week, she checked the mail. Sitting on her couch, she sorted through the mail. Most of it was junk mail and bills. But one thing stood out to her. It was an envelope addressed to her by a man named Ken. As far as she knew, she didn't know a Ken. Ripping it open, she started to read.

Immediately, she groaned and rolled her eyes. The damn door-to-door bible thumper had written her a letter all about accepting God to find her way. Why was this crazy man writing her a letter? Who did that? He stopped at her house to preach and when she couldn't talk, he took it upon himself to write to her. It was the weirdest thing she had ever seen. Other people had knocked to tell her about the good word, but no one had ever sent her a letter. But she saw no harm in throwing the letter away. The man would never know she did. If he ever came back around, she would not answer the door. Simple as that. Unfortunately, for Cassie, it would never be that simple.

The next few days went ahead without incident. She expected another letter in the mail or a knock at the door. Neither came. Relieved, Cassie felt she had finally rid herself of the man. The following night, Cassie sat watching television when her phone chirped with a text notification. Cassie reached for the phone and swiped up to read the message. For a few seconds, she was confused. The number was unknown, but it was addressed to her directly.

Hey Cassie, I hope all is well. I wanted to check in and see how you were doing. Hopefully, you've had a chance to look over that pamphlet that I left you. If you have any questions about anything, feel free to send me a text or call me. God bless.

Cassie's blood turned ice cold. Ken had texted her. But how? She never gave him her phone number; of that she was sure. What kind of creep searched for a person's phone number and text them without their permission? Especially a stranger who had only knocked on her door once. The letter had been weird, but this topped it for sure. It was creepy and Cassie felt unsafe. Though the man seemed to have no ill will, it was still a strange and scary thing to endure. If he could find her phone number, what else could he do?

For several minutes, she struggled with what to do. She wanted to respond and tell the man to leave her alone. Texting her without asking for her phone number was over the line. How could someone think that was okay? Especially, for a strange man to do that to a single woman. It only seemed like harassment. She could see no other way to explain it.

Eventually, she settled on deleting the text and pretending it never happened. If she never responded, maybe he would get the hint and leave her alone. After pressing delete, she wondered if she should have blocked the number instead. She decided it wasn't necessary. Ken would most likely never text again.

Cassie was wrong. Ken did text again. This time, it had nothing to do with the pamphlet or Jesus or anything. It was bizarre. Cassie wasn't sure if she should delete the text and block the number or call the police and have the man committed. He surely seemed to be out of his mind. She couldn't make a clear thought out of the text message.

"Mad me makes it. Me ignore people when it like don't I. That done hadn't you wish I. Trash the in pamphlet my threw you and message text my ignored you," the text read. She scanned it over and over, looking for any sort of sense. It was gibberish.

Cassie had picked out keywords like ignore, pamphlet, trash, and text. She thought she understood the gist of what it was saying. Ken was mad that she ignored his text message and threw away his pamphlet. Only, how did he know she threw it away? Her blood ran cold when she realized the man was watching her.

Pulling her phone to her eyes, she typed out the words I'm calling the police. Before she could hit send, the man's text caught her eye again. This time, she realized there was a complete thought written out before it. Ken had sent the text backward! Bizarre behavior indeed. You ignored my text message and you threw my pamphlet in the trash. I wish you hadn't done that. I don't like it when people ignore me. It makes me mad.

Now that she could read the text, she gasped. It sounded like a threat if ever she heard one. She was calling the police now. Pressing send on the text, Cassie switched over to the dial pad and pressed 911. It rang for less than a second before a monotone voice broke over the end. Before Cassie could speak, a gloved hand wrapped around her mouth. She let out a muffled cry, hoping the dispatcher would hear her. A second gloved hand grabbed her cell phone and pressed end call.

"In a few seconds, your phone is going to ring again. It will be the police. They always call back when you hang up. You're going to tell them you accidentally dialed and panicked, hanging up before you thought they would answer. If you say anything else, I will kill you."

She didn't need to turn around to know who it was. Somehow, Ken had broken into her home and now held her hostage. Tears ran down her cheeks when the phone rang again. He had been right. They were calling back. Ken handed the cell phone over and removed the hand from her mouth. He stood close by as she slid the green indicating, answering the call.

"H-hello?" She answered, trying to sound scared.

"Ma'am, we received a call from this number and a hang-up. Is everything okay?"

Cassie struggled. She wanted to tell the dispatcher nothing was okay. There was a man in her home with what she assumed was a knife pressed against her back. If she said anything to alert the police, she would be dead. She had every reason to believe the man.

"Oh, yeah, I did. Uh, sorry about that," she said. "It was, uh, an accident. Uh, I was hoping to hang up before you, uh, answered."

She pleaded with the dispatcher on the other end to sense something was wrong. Hear it in her speech pattern. Something was off. She had to hear it. Cassie begged God in her mind to send this woman a message.

"Ma'am, if you're in a position where you can't say anything but you're in danger, say you're sorry to have disturbed us."

Cassie couldn't blurt out the words fast enough. Thank God, the person on the other end had sensed the danger she was in. Cassie nearly yelled, "I'm sorry to disturb you."

"I understand. I will have police dispatch to your location right- "

Ken snatched the phone from her hand and smashed it beneath his boot. Cassie turned around the face the man, hoping he had not heard the other end of the conversation. The look on his face told her he had.

"Why did you have to go and do something like that? You could have been the one. But now, I have to end it here."

"Please, just leave me alone," Cassie screamed. "The police are on their way. If you run now, you might get away. Please, go!"

Ken stared at her with a wild look in his eyes. Spittle hung from his lips and his eyes glossed over like he had drifted to some distant memory. Cassie took the opportunity to run. Within seconds, the man gave chase. As Cassie ran for the front door, she dared a glance behind her. The man galloped on all fours like a cheetah. He snarled and screamed at her like a wild animal. Cassie screamed and bolted out of the house. She felt her lungs would burst as she ran into the street and cried for help.

A neighbor across the street ripped open their front door to see what the matter was. He saw the bizarre scene and immediately rushed to Cassie's aid, but it was too late. Ken had leaped an impossible distance and tackled the woman to the ground. He dug his teeth into her shoulder and tore flesh from bone. Cassie screamed out in pain as the neighbor rushed towards Ken.

He tackled the wild man to the ground, but it had been a mistake. Ken rammed both hands into the soft part of the neighbor's stomach and ripped it open. The neighbor staggered for a moment before collapsing on the ground. Ken whipped his head back towards Cassie and smiled. Blood oozed from her wound and she crawled backward away from Ken.

"I think I was wrong," he said. "You taste like the one." Ken pounced again.

When the police arrived a few minutes later, they found a pool of blood and the body of her neighbor. All signs of Cassie or her attacker were gone. Forensics found nothing at the crime scene. Her face was plastered all over the news and manhunts were conducted to find her or at least her remains. But nothing was ever found. Though, one person did eventually see Cassie again. Except, she didn't recognize her as the missing woman. It had been several months since Cassie's face had graced television screens. Blair smiled at the woman standing in her doorway holding a pamphlet in her hand.

"Excuse me," the woman said. "Do you have a moment to talk about your salvation?"

The Hooded Figure

The glow of the streetlights illuminated the quiet neighborhood, cutting through the darkness. Raccoons sifted through open trash cans, small rabbits hopped through dew-covered grass, and bats feasted on the insects fluttering under the streetlights. The scene was serene and nothing out of the ordinary. Except for the hooded figure standing alone on the sidewalk.

It stared at a house tucked away in a corner. No light emanated from any windows and the nearest streetlamp cast a dim glow on the driveway. Darkness draped over the silent home like a sheet. The hooded figure liked it that way.

For another thirty minutes, the figure stood in the darkness. The dark black hood shrouded the figure rendering it almost invisible. Curious eyes looking from bedroom windows would miss the figure. Darkness was its camouflage.

The hooded figure tilted its head to listen to the noises around it. The chirping of nocturnal insects had ceased. It was the telltale sign of what was coming. When the streetlights began to flicker, the hooded figure knew the being was close. Darkness was the being's domain and followed everywhere it went. It was the reason the hooded figure was so comfortable in the dark.

A streetlight at the end of the road popped and went out. A few seconds later, the next did the same. One by one, each streetlight popped and draped darkness over the neighborhood. Finally, the one nearest to the hooded figure went out. The being was finally close, though the hooded figure still could not see it. But that was alright. The hooded figure wasn't waiting to ambush it in the street. It could only be seen when it was close to its prey.

A heavy breeze rushed through the street and ruffled the hood obscuring the figure's face. It meant the being had moved passed and was planning its next move. Now was the time for the hooded figure to move. Carefully, the hooded figure stepped into the street. The last thing it wanted to do was alert the being to its presence. Once it was certain the coast was clear, the hooded figure moved quicker.

The being was most likely already in the home. Things like locks and doors couldn't keep it out. The same was true for the hooded figure. It walked up the driveway with caution and purpose, stopping only for a moment at the front door. No noise came from inside the house which meant the being had not fulfilled its purpose yet. There was still time.

Although the knob and deadbolt were both locked, the hooded figure pushed it open with ease. It was as if the locks had disengaged themselves at his presence. And once the door shut, it was back to normal. The hooded figure did not question this at all. For it, this was normal. As was chasing the being now somewhere in the house.

The hooded figure stepped lightly so it would not alert the being to its presence. Of course, it wasn't afraid to wake the family living in the house. It could choose to not be heard if it felt like it. At least, when it came to humans. The being wouldn't fall for those tricks.

As it moved, the hooded figure could feel faint vibrations of molecules. The being had been here recently. It stepped through the living room. Now, a thin trail of light bent and curved through the house, leading up the flight of stairs before the figure. When the being was close enough, these faint lighted trails acted as waypoint. It would lead straight to the being.

The hooded figure followed the white wisp in the air and made its way upstairs. The being could be heard, now. A faint growling pierced the silence. It came out as a continuous hum, like the sound of a muffled engine or air conditioning unit. The hum would blend in with the white noise around it. Humans would be unaware of its presence until it struck.

The figure turned the corner and stared down the dark corridor. There it was. A repulsive creature on all fours with an elongated head and long whipping tail. Every inch of the creature was as black as the night sky, rendering it almost invisible to the naked eye. But the hooded figure did not have any issue seeing the being for it was not human.

A massive, clawed paw stepped forward and into the bedroom of a sleeping girl no more than seven. The being had come to grip the child in its gaping maw and drag her back to its lair. There it would feast on her anguish until there was nothing left. Then she would be cast aside into eternal darkness. Lost for all eternity. But the hooded figure wouldn't allow it. It had stopped several beings before and it would stop this one.

The dark black mass stepped into the room and the hooded figure followed close behind it. Before the being could approach the bed, the hooded figure placed a firm foot on its tail. The being howled and turned to face its new prey. The hooded figure took a large step back into the hallway. The being barred its teeth and advanced. Oblivious to it all, the little girl slept in her bed with her hands wrapped around her pillow.

Drool hung from the being's jaws as it snapped at the hooded figure. Flecks of spittle rained out, leaving the only physical evidence of the being's existence. Still walking backward, the hooded figure made its way towards the front door. Once there, it opened for him like it had when he entered. Luckily, the being was still interested in its new prey and followed.

Once the two were outside, the hooded figure knew it could finally make its move. Fighting with the being inside would have been dangerous for the occupants. At least outside, there would be little chance of collateral damage. Especially this late at night.

The being lunged at the hooded figure with its mouth wide open. The hooded figure managed to dodge the strike and the being's mouth snapped shut only inches away. The tail whipped around and smacked the figure with great force. Landing hard on the ground, the hooded figure rolled over and stood up. The tip of the tail began to change. It no longer looked like an ordinary animal's tail but now had a pointed end like the tip of a dagger. The being dragged the blade across its skin causing black blood to trickle to the ground.

As the being charged again, the bladed tail sliced the air, almost cutting the figure's chest. The figure's gloved hand caught hold of the tail and bent it backward. The being yelped in surprise and tried to pull away, but the figure's grip was too strong. It pulled the creature back with all its might and gripped the creature at the base of the tail. The being flailed its mighty paws but could not hit the figure at the angle at which the figure held it.

The hooded figure flung its head so the hood fell back. It revealed the features of a smooth head, like that of a mannequin. Its skin seemed to be made of a shiny, black substance like oil. The black sheen glistened in the starlight above. Pulling the tail closer, the hooded figure touched the being's tail to its featureless face. Then the being began to melt like an ice cube. Instead of dripping to the ground below, large globs of the being floated through the air. The figure's skin absorbed these globs like a sponge.

As the hooded figure stood there, its oily skin rippled like the surface of a pond. Once the rippling stopped, the figure reached for the hood in an attempt to pull it back up over its smooth features. It knew to hide from the world as humans would only fear it. Though, they had nothing to fear for it was a protector of the human race. These beings came from a place between the fabric of existence and fed off human misery and despair. The hooded figure hunted these creatures and absorbed their essence, destroying them forever.

Something moved in the window of the house the figure had left and it looked up. There in the window stood the little girl who had almost met her demise that night. She stared at the being, unblinking. If she was afraid of his smooth, featureless face she did not act it. If the figure had human-like features, it would have smiled at the little girl and produced a wink. It had seen other humans do it before. All it could manage to do was hold up a gloved hand and wave. The little girl smiled as if she knew the hooded figure had been there to help and not hurt. The hooded figure loved children. They unknowingly had a sense for these sorts of things. An adult would have assumed the worst. That it was some sort of murderer or molester come to torture the family. Of course, the figure couldn't blame them as human beings were worse to each other than the creatures it hunted. But it was refreshing to be looked upon and not feared.

With a step backward, the hooded figure disappeared into the darkness. The little girl stood in the window for some time, scanning the ground for any trace of it. When she was certain it had gone, the little girl tip-toed back to bed. An image of the shiny figure danced in her mind, but she would forget it by morning.

The Eyes

I am telling this tale to the best of my recollection. No longer having the audio files that I stumbled across, I must do my best to tell you this story from memory. For me, it started on a hiking trip through the Florida Everglades. Camping and hiking are passions of mine. I'm outdoors any chance I can get. A couple of months ago, I went backpacking and camped in some of the primitive sites the park has to offer. Feeling a little adventurous, I went off trail for a few nights.

Normally, going off-trail is a bad idea, especially in the Everglades. Several people have been lost there, never to be seen again. Not to mention, the myriad of dangerous animals like alligators and crocodiles.

I was fine. But during one of the nights camping off-trail, I came across a small clearing that looked like it had been used as a campsite before. There was a small hole in the ground with dusty embers inside. Other than a few small pieces of trash, it was empty. I thought I had missed the campers by mere days.

I pulled the tent out of my bag and set it up in the middle of the clearing and used the already dug hole as my fire pit. Collecting a decent amount of firewood, I settled in for the night. Nothing of major importance happened that night but in the morning I stumbled across something...*strange.*

A few feet away from the fire pit, I found another patch of disturbed Earth. Removing the small, orange shovel-usually reserved for restroom purposes-I uncovered a green plastic box. Opening it, I found an audio recorder inside. It was strange but I didn't think too much of it. Grabbing the recorder, I pressed play.

I was greeted by the sound of a man describing some sort of ecological trip they were conducting. It seemed like research notes of some kind. Interested, I scooped the recorder up and dropped it in my pack. Placing the box back in the hole, I broke down my site and continued on my way.

Like I said before, nothing of importance happened on this trip. It was when I got home I found out how disturbing the files were. I will now recount the audio that I found on those files to the best of my ability and hopefully in the correct order.

"This is Dr. Alan Crane with Cathy Cumberland," the male voice on the recorder said. "We are documenting this trip with audio devices to better gather our research." I could hear shuffling around as if some papers were being pushed aside.

"Hey, don't touch that," said a female voice that I assumed was Cathy Cumberland.

"I need the space for my recorder. You want to get everything documented, right?"

"Yes, but-"

"Now, now. Don't give me any lip."

"Shut the hell up, Alan."

It was obvious the pair didn't get along. I wondered why it was they were working together. Then the male voice spoke again, "Ah, and this is my intern Laura."

"You mean *my* intern," Cathy shouted.

"Nope, mine," Alan whispered to the device. "Say hi, Laura."

A shy voice in the distance said hello.

"She is coming with us on this expedition to learn more about our particular field. Care to explain what it is we are studying, Laura?"

She mumbled something about audio experimentation but seemed too shy to continue. Alan pulled the recorder away and pressed it close to his face saying, "That's ok, I'll explain it since I'm the only one here who *really* understands it."

I don't quite remember exactly how he explained it, a lot of it went over my head. But from what I could gather, they were studying levels of what they referred to as "sound pollution" deep in the Everglades. I guess there was a theory that sound produced by modern society was causing a shift in the ecosystem. Certain animals were no longer found in their normal habitats near busy cities and instead traveled deeper into the woods. This sets off a chain reaction in the ecosystem and throws a lot of it out of sync. Animals that were normally nocturnal have been found hunting during the day and so on. From what it sounded like, they were planning to take a backpacking trip into the Everglades with audio equipment. The goal was to take "samples" to see how the audio levels were affecting the ecosystem.

Not much happened in the first audio file. Alan talked more about the expedition and the type of data they would be collecting. I remember he spoke in a sort of arrogant way, almost as if he thought he was the smartest person in the room. I could tell his colleague, Cathy, didn't take kindly to this and they hardly ever got along.

In the second audio file, Alan was introducing another man by the name of Sean. Apparently, he was an entomologist. "State your name and profession for the record please," Alan said into the recorder.

"My name is Sean Whitcomb. I'm an entomologist."

"Bug scientist, in layman terms," Alan teased.

"Sure, you can call it that."

"And why are you tagging along with us on this trip? "

"To collect data about local insect species and how their patterns are disrupted at night due to audio vibrations caused by neighboring geographical locations of the human variety."

"In other words, to see if the bugs get pissed at the loud noises from cities." Alan joked.

"Correct."

He seemed like a shy guy as well. He and Laura the intern would probably get along. Farther along on the files, one last person was introduced. Again, Alan asked him to state his name and profession and why he was there for the "expedition record."

"I'm Brian Hunt, zoologist. I guess I'm doing the same thing everyone else is. Studying the local ecosystem where animals are concerned."

"That's right, folks," Alan interrupted. "We have an animal scientist, bug scientist, my intern, and two acousticians. We're heading out into the Everglades with our expensive equipment to study audio patterns and have the zoologist and entomologist here to compare their data with ours."

He spoke sarcastically as if he didn't like the others tagging along. I figured it was because he felt he could do a better job all by himself, but maybe it was because he had a thing for his colleague, Cathy, and saw the other two men as a threat.

The rest of the audio followed the group preparing for the trip and heading out in one vehicle together. There was a lot of banter during the drive out. I think Alan was recording most of the trip without everyone's knowledge. I'm not sure why he wanted all of it recorded, but maybe he just really liked to hear himself talk.

Regardless, nothing of any major importance happened until the next audio file. They had camp all set up and night was falling. Their audio equipment had been set up deep in the woods, far from their campsite. Alan must have flipped his recorder back on and I heard them sitting around a crackling campfire talking and telling stories. Alan told some stupid story about the Florida Skunk Ape. I remember Brian, the zoologist, laughing about it and telling him why the animal didn't exist.

It was around this time something happened that terrified me. Cathy said she was going to hike out to the audio equipment to make sure everything was running properly before heading off to bed. None of the others decided to go with her, probably not wanting to make the trip out there. Cathy didn't seem worried, however, and headed off by herself. I listened to this part so many times, wishing I could tell her to turn around. I begged she wouldn't find whatever it was she found out there.

The ones left at camp, save for Laura who had gone off to bed, sat around the fire still talking. I can't remember what it was they were talking about, but I remember the scream. It was a blood-curdling cry unlike any other I had ever heard in my life. What was weird, was it seemed to cut off as if the sound itself had been plucked out of the air. It was Cathy.

Alan must have grabbed the recorder and slipped it into his pocket. Then next few minutes all I could hear was muffled shuffling around and what sounded like booming footsteps on the ground as if he were running. Finally, the recorder was pulled out of the pocket and I heard Alan say, "Cathy, what the hell is wrong? What are you looking at?"

She mumbled something that I couldn't hear and Alan asked again. "Please, turn around and tell us what you saw. A bear or something?"

"A bear out here would be highly unli-" Brian started but Alan cut him off.

"No one cares, man. Cathy, what the hell was it?"

Finally, I could hear Cathy turn around but what she was saying made no sense.

"Darkness, utter darkness like I've never seen before. Green glowing orbs and *silence.* Oh god, the silence. I couldn't even hear my own thoughts!"

"If you're pulling a prank on us, it's not funny," Brian said.

Then something happened that was unnerving. The sounds of the woods around them ceased. The cicadas that chirped, the branches that swayed in the wind, and even the faint chirps of bats as they fed stopped. All at once, there was silence.

"What the hell?" Sean asked, noticing the change in sound. Then a noise broke over the recorder. It was utterly terrifying. It sounded like all of the sounds of the woods concentrated into one single wave of audio blasted in a stream like someone had weaponized sound itself. I could hear them all scream and begin to run.

They ran until they made it back to camp. Breathless, Alan said, "What the *fuck* was that thing?"

"I've never seen anything like it before," Brian said.

"Cathy, is that what you saw out there? Is that why you screamed?" Alan asked.

I heard a soft yes in return.

"What the fuck?" Sean screamed. "It was like a shadow. Nothing but darkness. An outline of a person. You guys saw that, right?"

"Yes," Alan said. "But what about the eyes?"

"Green orbs!" Brian shouted. "Just like Cathy said."

"It absorbed the sound, everything. How the hell could it do that? I've never heard of anything that can do that," Alan rambled.

They went on talking about the creature in hushed, terrified tones for a few more minutes. From their descriptions, I learned it was a tall, humanoid figure. Maybe about eight feet tall. It was completely dark, with no color whatsoever. I pictured a shadow with a mind of its own. But it had bright green eyes that glowed like little spotlights in the middle of its pitch-black head. They said it could absorb sound in the area and push it forward in a focused cone of energy.

"Get Laura out of her tent," Alan screamed. "We're getting the fuck out of here."

There was rustling and the sound of a tent being opened and then...

"Laura," Alan began shouting. "She's not in her tent. Where could she be."

My blood ran cold when I heard another scream on the file. It was Laura. Much like Cathy, it was loud and all at once silenced. Everyone began to talk over each other. I couldn't understand a word. When the sounds of the forest slowly receded, I knew something was wrong. Desperately, I screamed at my computer screen for the group to run but they just stood there, questioning.

God, the silence was strange. All the sounds of the forest stopped in an instant. There was nothing. It shook me to my very core. As I waited for the inevitable wave of sound to return, a terrible thought crossed my mind. Whatever had happened on these files happened where I had camped only a few nights before. Whatever it was that attacked these people could have come after me. At least, I thought. Maybe the group had found a way to defeat it. I had to get to the end. I had to know what happened.

The blast of sound did return and the audio file clicked off. I think the rest of the file was corrupted. Before it ended, however, there was this odd mechanical hiss. It reminded me of the sound an old cassette tape made when the film got caught.

Trying to listen to the next file, I found it was corrupted as well. I was frantic. I wanted to know what was happening. I clicked on the next file and crossed my fingers. It started with the sound of a man sobbing. I recognized it as Alan. Leaves shuffled underneath him as he moved.

"It took them," he cried. "There was sound and darkness and then they were gone. All of them." He continued to sob. "I tried to save them. I think it's coming back for me."

Again, the sounds of the woods stopped. I could hear Alan jump to his feet and start running, panting as he went. He tried to explain what was happening, but I couldn't understand him. He ran for the remainder of the file. When it ended, I quickly played the next.

"I think we lost it," Brian was saying. I realized this file was out of order. From what I could gather, they ran shortly after being blasted by the sound wave. Laura wasn't with them. They had left her out there. Left her to the fate of that *thing*. I guess I didn't blame them.

There wasn't much of importance on this file. The group mostly walked and talked about the being they had seen. They argued about which way was out, and which way was back. The last thing on the file was the sound of silence once again. It had returned.

Only one file remained. I doubled-clicked it and listened to the distressed voice of Alan. “I’m the only one left,” he stammered. “It’s coming back for me, I can feel it. I stumbled across our camp again. I’ve been trying to get out of these god damned woods for hours and I was walking in a fucking circle.” He laughed. “Perfect.”

I heard the sound of something unzipping. I figured it was his pack.

“I’m going to bury this recorder. I know I won’t make it out of these woods. If someone should stumble across these, know what happened here. I don’t know if they’re dead but they’re all gone. Brian, Sean, Laura, and Cathy. It took them all. It was like a cloud of black smoke. It circled them. When the black fog cleared, they were gone. It took them one by one until only I was left. It’s going to take me too. No matter where I go, it will find me. I don’t know how I know that, I just do. Even if I made it out of these woods tonight, it would eventually find me.”

My hands were shaking as I listened. I couldn’t believe something like this was happening. This shit didn’t happen, did it? Maybe in movies but not real life.

“To the person who finds this recorder, get away from here. Run. Don’t stop until you get out of these woods. If you happen upon this, this *thing,* don’t look it in the eyes. Those green orbs are the death of you!”

With that, the file ended and that was it. There was nothing else. Dumbfounded, I looked up the people from the recordings. All of them are missing. Their equipment had been found in the woods. The sensitive audio equipment they had used had all been scrambled. It seemed the only thing that had survived the attack was the recorder.

I had planned to take the recorder to the police. I thought they should hear what was on it. Maybe they could figure out what the hell was in the woods that night. Maybe they were all out there still and had a chance, though somehow, I knew it wasn’t true. They were most likely gone. I locked the recorder away in my desk and went to bed, terrified to dream of the creature.

When I awoke in the morning, the recorder was gone. The desk was locked but the recorder was no longer in it. I have no fucking clue where the damn thing went. What’s worse, the audio files I had copied to my computer were gone too. Any proof I had that some creature had taken that group of people was gone. Who had taken it? In my mind, there was only one explanation. It was the creature. It had come for the proof of its existence. Does it know about me? Will it be watching *me* now?

I sit here now, writing this here. No one else would believe but I figured you all might. It's been a day since the recorder went missing. Thinking that I only misplaced it, I tore my house apart. It wasn't there. I think it wants to come for me. Last night, the noise outside my bedroom window stopped. I buried my face in the pillow and stayed that way all night. Whatever happens, I will do my best to never look it in the eyes.

The Drive

Gary went for a morning drive. It was a beautiful day and he wanted to get out of the house. For the past couple of weeks, he had been cooped up. He needed fresh air and he needed sunlight. Besides, driving always helped him relax and clear his mind. With the gorgeous blue sky above, Gary set out on his miniature adventure.

As he aimlessly drove, he let his mind wander. Gary didn't think about anything in particular. Random thoughts fluttered through his mind. He let them drift to wherever they took him. It was nice to relax and not have to think for a while. He continued to drive through the small town he lived in and took in all the sights.

There wasn't much to see where he was from. It was a small town in the middle of nowhere. Most people driving around were passing through. There wasn't much of a reason to stop. They didn't have any theme parks or local attractions. Despite this, the roads always seemed to be quite busy. But Gary didn't mind. He just enjoyed the drive.

An image flashed into his mind of something he had never seen before. He could see it as clear as day. It was a run-down neighborhood with boarded-up windows and peeling paint. Gary had to shake his head to stop the visions. Whether it was a hallucination or a vision, he couldn't tell. But now something else was happening that he couldn't explain. Like an animal on pure instinct, he started driving towards an unknown destination.

It was the strangest sensation. There was no conscious decision on which way to drive. He turned in a certain direction when he had a feeling. And he didn't know why he was doing it. Gary was certain he wouldn't be able to stop even if he wanted to. Part of him wanted to know where he was going.

Then he heard a strange whisper in his ear like someone had leaned over from the passenger seat. He couldn't make it out the first time but when it spoke again, he did. It was a low whisper, more like a hiss of a snake. Gary may have imagined it, but he thought he could feel hot breath on his ear.

"Arrive," the voice whispered.

For some unknown reason, he wanted to find the source of the voice. The voice was calling out to him and he needed to find out why. None of this was normal but Gary was beyond questioning. He was being compelled to find this location and to find the voice. There was a purpose in his life now. He didn't know what that purpose was but he was anxious to find out.

Now, the drive couldn't have been any longer. He wanted to speed down the road towards his unknown destination. But getting pulled over by the police wouldn't get him there any faster. So, he obeyed the traffic laws and continued on his way. He would be there soon enough. Then, all of his questions would be answered.

Gary was nearing a part of town he rarely ever came to. Despite not knowing where he was, he navigated the streets with ease. It felt like he had grown up on these very streets. Every direction felt like a memory now. He could see the decaying neighborhood in his mind's eye better now. Something about it looked and felt familiar. Like an extreme case of déjà vu, he could remember the neighborhood but not remember from where. He hoped he could remember if he thought hard enough but nothing came to him. Only the image and the feeling remained. Gary shrugged, hoping he would know sooner rather than later.

The hot breath appeared on his ear again. When he turned to face it, there was nothing there. For the first time, fear welled up inside of Gary but he didn't waver. He continued on his path, needing to know where it would lead him. When the hot breath returned, it came back with another word.

"Here," the voice said.

Arrive. Here. So far, he could tell what the voice was telling him to do. It wanted him to arrive at the place he had seen. If only the voice had whispered why. But he supposed that would ruin everything including the mystery. The idea of not knowing why he was being summoned to this place was electrifying. He had never done anything like this in his life and it felt amazing. His very own adventure. Of course, no one would ever believe him if he told him. And anyone who might believe him would probably have him committed. He couldn't say he would blame them. Hearing voices, seeing hallucinations, driving to a place you've never seen before because the voices told you to. It all sounded crazy.

This was the sanest he had ever felt. There was a certain clarity to his thoughts now. Something in his mind was becoming clearer the farther he drove. He didn't know what, exactly, that was but he would know soon. He was sure of it. When he reached this mysterious neighborhood, he would know everything he needed to.

The voice broke out over his ear again. This time it whispered *with*. Arrive. Here. With. Those three words were spelling out a sentence. What was he supposed to arrive with? Was he supposed to bring an offering of some type? He didn't know what to bring. He hoped the voice would tell him before he arrived. No part of him wanted to mess this up.

He was close now. He could feel it. He had turned down a long stretch of road which ended in a dead end. At the end of this road, he would find his destination, he was sure of it. The trees began to envelop the road around him, casting him in a shade. The hot breath returned to his ear. It let out sharp breaths for several seconds before disappearing.

There was excitement in the voice. Gary was excited as well. Finally, he had reached his destination and would know just what was happening. Fantasies of all sorts raced through his mind. Everything from being granted god-like abilities to finding a lost secret that would make him rich. There was no telling what would come next.

The dilapidated buildings could be seen now. They sat on the side of the road, neglected for years. He wondered about their story. Who had lived there and for how long? Why did they leave? Would he learn these secrets as well? He could only hope so.

Before his eyes, a whole abandoned neighborhood appeared. There were windows boarded up, doors bolted shut, and paint peeling from the exteriors. It was the neighborhood from his vision. He was finally there! He had reached his destination.

Though, he noticed the voice had become silent. He had expected it to speak again once he had arrived. It had been instructing him to arrive all this time and now that he was there, it had nothing to say. It made no sense. Gary wondered if there was a delay. Whatever force had been leading him was busy or distracted.

Now, with control back over his actions, Gary decided to keep driving around the neighborhood until something happened. He would take in the sights around him. Gary had never explored an abandoned location before so this would be fun. He admired his surroundings, wondering about the story these buildings could tell. There was once a community here and he tried to picture it. He imagined cars parked in the driveways, clothes hung up on clotheslines, and grills giving off a delicious aroma in backyards. Gary could almost see the kids chasing each other through the grass while playing tag.

Then he noticed he could hear it all around him as well. Somehow, the daydream of a community had come alive in his head. He could smell the air. He could hear the children. It was all real in his mind. Somewhere, the sweet smell of grilled steak hung in the air. He could even smell the chlorine of the pool. As he drove around, he wondered if these were in his mind or if they were somehow a memory. It all seemed too familiar to be a hallucination. Gary could have sworn he had been here before. This sight, these sounds, everything about this seemed familiar. But he had never lived here before, he was sure of it.

Like a brick wall, the memory slammed into him. He almost passed out at the vivid recollection of the memory now. He had lived here, many years ago. This place had been his home. The image in his mind wasn't a conjured up one but something he had experienced long ago. But now, a more disturbing image came to mind. Images of blood and dead bodies flashed through his mind. There were dismembered body parts strewn about living rooms. People cried as they begged for their lives.

A plague had ripped through this community years ago. Gary had been that plague. He had ripped through the neighborhood at night, killing as many people as he could before vanishing altogether. Those who had survived fled the day after. With dozens of their neighbors hacked up in the middle of the night, it seemed Satan himself had made residence on the block.

Gary brought the car to a stop and stared for a moment. He could remember it all now. The coppery smell of the blood as he murdered anyone he could. Somehow, the memories had become lost to him. But now they poured over him like a river. He had forgotten about the hot breath when it suddenly boomed in his ear yelling, "*US!*"

Arrive. Here. With. Us.

Sitting next to him, he saw a spirit form. He remembered the face clearly as one of the women he had hacked up that night. She stared at him with vengeance in her eyes. More spirits started to arrive inside the car and all around it. At that moment, he realized why he had been called back. His victims were angry, and they wanted their revenge.

Watching

I watch you every day, but you never know I'm there. I know everything there is to know about you. It's amazing what you can learn about someone by digging through their trash. With everything that I've learned about you, I still want to know more. Of course, I know what you look like but I want to know what you feel like. Is your skin soft and delicate? What do your lips taste like? Are they soft and luscious?

You have no idea who I am, but I want that to change. I want to introduce myself to you but I'm afraid. I'm afraid you won't like me for who I am. Or you will think I'm a hideous monster. I can admit, I'm not the most normal of people. But I have no ill intent, I promise you. I'm just shy. I've never been with a woman and sometimes I'm afraid I never will.

Most women don't even give me a second glance. Any that do, I end up running from. I'm too afraid to strike up a conversation. The only way I can ever get close is like I am now. Hiding outside your home, watching you from afar. The more I watch you, the more courage I get to knock on your door and ask you out to dinner. But how would I ever explain that? I've been watching you; would you like to go on a date? I know women don't like that sort of thing.

Which leaves me only this one option. To watch you. To keep you in my sights. To protect you at all costs. I'm afraid there are people out there that would want to hurt you. At least with me out here, I know they will never get to you. Could I tell you that? Would that make you feel better about me watching you? I'm not sure.

You are so beautiful and I'm certain I'm in love with you. I know, I know. How can I be in love with someone I've never met? You just have this certain way about you. Everything you do is amazing. From the way you sing to yourself while cleaning the dishes to how you dance when vacuuming the house. You are adorable when you think no one is watching. But I'm always here, watching you.

In my mind, we have all sorts of fun together. We do everything together. Everything from watching Netflix in our underwear to traveling the world together. It's only a daydream now but I'm sure it will come true one day. You and I are meant to be. You just haven't figured it out yet, that's all. And I'm not mad at you for that.

I don't want there to be any secrets between us. So, in the spirit of honesty, I have to admit something to you. While you were showering a few weeks ago, I did sneak into your home. Yes, I know it was wrong. I shouldn't come in uninvited. But I had to experience your home for myself. I had to know what it smelled like, you know? I always pictured it smelling like cherry blossom, which is your favorite lotion. I couldn't pinpoint the smell but it was lovely. Something fruity and wonderful.

If you ask me, I showed incredible restraint. After all, the love of my life was in the other room showering. I could hear the water splashing off your body. It took every ounce of willpower to not ask if I could join you. But I didn't, in the end. I left your house and went back to my usual spot. I watched your silhouette through the opaque glass as you toweled off. One day, you would notice me and I would be able to join you. For now, I was happy to watch from afar.

When you went on vacation, I was sad. The love of my life was gone for a whole week. It was a depressing week for me. The only thing to get me through was sleeping in your bed. Oh, I should probably admit again that I snuck into your home while you were gone. I promise, there was no ill intent. I was there to keep your house safe while you were out. I kept some lights on at night so people would think you were still home. The idea of you coming home to a robbed house filled me with anxiety.

My god, your bed is comfortable. And your pillow still smells like you even when you're gone. I think it was the best sleep of my life. I cuddled up against your pillow and held it tight, wishing it was you. That night, I dreamt sweet dreams of you. We had a house together and a family. It was the perfect life. You loved me exactly the way I am. Waking up that morning was difficult. Knowing you weren't there depressed me. But spending the day in your homemade up for it. I've never spent so much time there.

After spending a week in your home, I felt closer to you. The relationship I had always wanted with you seemed closer than ever. My wildest dreams were coming true. So, you can imagine my surprise when you brought home another man after your trip. I had never seen this guy before. So, of course, I grew worried for you. This guy could have been a creep!

He seemed to be moving into your house with you. How could this be? You weren't meant to be with him. You're meant to be with me. This betrayal hurt. I know, it's hard to blame you when you don't even know I exist. But still, our love is true love and you shouldn't have eyes for anyone else. You should feel like I do, that he's not the one for you. But it didn't seem like you were getting that feeling. Which meant, this new man had to go.

For the first time in a long time, I didn't follow you to work. Instead, I followed him. I knew he was bad news. There was something wrong with this guy and I would prove it. That would be the way into your heart. I would be the man who showed you the unfaithful jerk you were with. You would be so grateful; we would start dating and life would be good.

As I suspected, this man of yours met with another woman for lunch. I could already feel the heartbreak you would soon go through. But it would all be for the best. The path you were on with this guy wasn't the one for you. You belonged with me. I watched as this man sat for an entire lunch date with this disgusting woman. It's not her fault, I suppose. She didn't know the type of man she was with, much like you.

I was going to get him out of your life. You would thank me for it one day. The only problem was, I didn't know how to do that. I would have taken a picture of this jerk with his side woman, but my phone was too old and not good enough. The photo would never come out. It left me with only one other option.

That afternoon, I followed the man back to your house. I was happy to see you weren't home yet. There was still no formal plan in my mind. I figured I would sneak into your house once more and scare the man away. I thought if I could run him away, it would spare you the heartache. But when I confronted him inside your home, he wasn't very receptive. I'm ashamed to say I had to hit him with something to get him off me. I think I hit him harder than I meant to because he didn't move after that. I panicked then. I didn't want you coming home to a dead body. What kind of first impression would that make?

I found an old tarp hidden away in your garage and wrapped the body up inside. Dragging it through the backyard and into the alley behind your house was difficult. But not as difficult as getting the body away from your home and buried. I won't even tell you what went into that. But believe me, it was daunting.

The next few days were hard to watch. Your tears broke my heart, but I knew it was for the best. Without that terrible man in your life, you would flourish. And more importantly, you would flourish with me at your side. It was only a matter of time. There is a hole in your heart that I would help fill.

I overheard you on the phone late last night. You had your bedroom windows open and I found a perfect place in some bushes in your backyard. You were crying. At first, I thought you were crying about the man who had run out on you. But it didn't take long to realize you had lost someone else in your life. I guess your brother went missing. I was sorry to hear that. Hopefully, his disappearance made you forget about that good-for-nothing boyfriend of yours. In light of recent events, I thought today would be the perfect day to introduce myself to you. You need me now more than ever. When we get together tonight, you'll forget all about that awful man and your missing brother. I'll make sure of it. I love you. See you soon.

Epilogue

A soft glow from smoldering embers radiates from a small clearing in the thick forest. Drenched in sweat, a man pushes through the underbrush. He cautiously enters the clearing, keeping his distance from the pile of ash before him. The man looks as though he has not had a hot meal or shower in weeks. Mud and dirt cake his face and body.

He takes in a deep breath and drops his pack to the ground. A great weight seems lifted from his shoulders as he stretches his arms towards the heavens, desperate for a chance to relax. A wind whips through the trees, taking with it a cloud of dust from the dying fire.

The traveler approaches the pit, picking up a nearby stick. He spots three piles of ash sitting around what was once a burning fire. Something had been sitting here earlier in the night. Had the traveler arrived sooner, perhaps he would have seen whatever it was. Now, all he saw were their charred remains.

Shrugging his shoulders, the traveler picks up his bag and slings it back over his shoulders. It's time to continue on his path. There is nothing for him here. He leaves the clearing and carries back on through the thick forest.

Acknowledgments

First and foremost, I must thank my friend Wofford Lee Jones for helping me put together the idea for this book. With his help, I was able to craft this book into something wonderful. His help bouncing ideas is always invaluable. And his contributions for artwork in the embers section of this book was incredible. He's an amazing author as well. Please consider checking him out at www.woffordleejones.com[1]

Second, I need to thank Brian Lee for some incredible artwork contributed to this book as well. Without his art, the embers section would have burned out. Instead, they glowed like hot burning coals. I really think it tied this whole book together! If you'd like to know where you can check out his art or give him a follow, check out his bio below:

Brian has created artwork using various mediums for over 50 years. He is particularly passionate about watercolor.

Brian's work reveals the use of lights and darks, as he focuses on capturing the natural beauty in an outdoor setting, creating shadowy effects in his paintings.

Brian sees a great sense of fulfillment in creating a good work of art, and always embraces the "happy accidents" which can occur in the painting process.

Brian lives in Greenville, SC and enjoys art, traveling, golfing, and taking walks with his wife Mary Sue.

Brian's Instagram is @brianlee0856. For display of his work, watch for his website which will appear on his Instagram at a future date.

I must always thank my wonderful patrons over on Patreon for supporting me and my writing journey. Roxie, Eileen, and Nicole. With your help, I'm able to continue crafting more and more books just like this one.

Let me also take a moment to thank anyone who read my work on sites like Simily, Vocal, and Ko-Fi of where many of these stories were first produced. Any comments or likes helped keep me creating more and more. So, a big thank you to everyone who read my work there.

1. http://www.woffordleejones.com

Of course, I wouldn't be a writer without awesome readers like you. To take the time to grab my book and read through to the end means so much to me. And if you're reading this, you're even cooler! Thanks for reading *Charred Remains* and please consider leaving a review on your favorite reading platform.

Now, I've got one more extra story for you. A bonus story, if you will. It's titled *Death Loves Her Balance* and it follows a spirit who hunts dangerous spirits for Death and was the basis for my upcoming book *After Death*. The book will be releasing later in 2022. So look out for that. You can always head to my website www.EvanBondAuthor.com[2] to sign up for my newsletter to see when that book will be releasing. Until then, please enjoy this extra special story!

2. http://www.EvanBondAuthor.com

Death Loves Her Balance

The engine roared like a lion guarding its prey as it tore down the long stretch of quiet road. The pale moonlight glinted off the puddles on the asphalt from a late-night shower. With one hand on the wheel, and the other hand holding a cigarette, Jeffrey cruised down the road. His metallic black Corvette Stingray flew like a missile. Propping his right knee against the steering wheel, Jeffrey flicked a bit of ash off of his black leather jacket.

Off in the distance, something white caught his eye. Letting off the accelerator, he slowed down enough to see it was a woman. She stood in a beam of moonlight which illuminated her pure, white dress. She wore nothing else. He smiled and pulled off to the side of the road. Extending his arm, he opened the passenger door and leaned over to speak with the woman.

"Hey there, lady," he said through his southern drawl. "Need a ride?"

The woman in white smiled a wide grin and climbed in the car. Jeffrey smiled and readjusted his mirror. She was a beautiful woman with a soft, pale face. Her long black hair flowed over her shoulders like a waterfall. Her white dress was impeccable, without a single stain or rip. It was odd for someone who had been hitchhiking all night.

"Whereyou headed?" he asked, pronouncing where and you as one word.

"To my home," she said, sounding distant and quiet. "It's only a few miles down the road."

Jeffrey smiled and pressed the accelerator harder. He was anxious to deliver her to her destination. The drive was short and silent, save for the growl of the engine. The woman in white pointed to a dirt road up ahead on the right. The path looked overgrown but Jeffrey was able to drive down the bumpy trail. A building materialized from the trees which looked like it had been abandoned ages ago. Shutters swung from rusted hinges. Cracks like spiderwebs covered the windows that were still intact. Rotten wood covered almost every inch of the home.

"This where you live?" Jeffrey asked, not sounding the least bit concerned.

The woman in white turned to him and nodded. Her hair rose and danced around her face like marionette dolls. The hem of her dress fluttered and moved on its own. A soft, white glow enveloped the woman as she leaned closer to Jeffrey. He smiled at her, not moving.

"Would you like to come inside?" She said, her voice sounding airy and resonate.

Jeffrey chuckled and nodded. This seemed to please the woman and she leaned closer, begging for a kiss. A breeze seemed to appear inside of the car, billowing around the two occupants. A thin fog began to rise around the property, making its way towards the car. It rolled over the hood and cascaded across the windshield, blocking their view. Jeffrey looked at the woman reaching for him, her lips parted for a kiss.

In an instant, her soft features turned ugly and vulgar. Her eyes sank into her head. The color drained from her smooth skin and turned a dark gray. It sagged from her bones like bags full of water. Her pupils expanded until they took up the entirety of her eyes, making them seem like pools of darkness. Her fingernails grew long and pointed, digging into the upholstery of her seat. The woman unhinged her jaw like a snake and opened wide, showing several rows of razor-sharp teeth. All this happened in the blink of an eye but Jeffrey remained unphased. The woman in white had never experienced this before. Most mortal men screamed and ran from their cars. She would play an enticing game of cat and mouse before killing them. Then she would leave their bodies to rot away along with the house. But something about this man was different. Blinking, she tried snarling at him but he only smirked.

Her features snapped back to the beautiful woman in white as she sat there, stunned. Jeffrey laughed and looked her in the eyes. He pulled a knife from his jeans pocket. It had a peculiar shape, curving outward. It looked more like the blade of a miniature scythe. Jeffrey met her gaze and pointed the tip in her direction.

"That's a cute trick. Bet it works on the fellas nicely," he said, pushing the blade towards her. She tried to pull the handle to let herself out of the car but it wouldn't budge. She found it impossible to phase through it, either. Her body had now taken on a near mortal mass. Something about the vehicle had changed her.

"Y'all find it impossible to escape, my dear," he said in his sweet, country accent. "The dead can't escape the dead." He looked at her now and his features began to change. What had once been a chiseled jawline with a hint of five o'clock shadow became a rotting, unhinged jaw. His hair became thin and ragged. Bugs crawled from each strand and into his ear canals. Rotted flesh pulled away from the bones, leaving behind clean white underneath. He no longer looked human. Instead, he resembled some undead nightmare.

"Tell ya what," He said, snapping back to the handsome man. "Since I respect your profession, and really, I do, I'll give ya a chance. I'll let y'all out of this car and give ya a chance to hide from me. If I can't find you by sunup, you go free. But, if I find ya, well, I'll plunge this knife into ya and... well, let's just say you won't be haunting anyone again."

Now, the woman in white laughed.

"You can't kill a ghost. I don't care how undead you are."

"Y'all see this knife? It's a special knife. Given to me by Death herself. With it, I can reap all the souls I want. I was a killer in life and now I'm a killer in death." He smirked. Before she could react, he sliced off her pinky finger and it dissolved into a fine mist. She screamed. It was the first time she had felt fear since before she could remember. She had been preying on hitchhikers for an eternity, it seemed.

"Three..," he started. "Two...One." With that, the doors unlocked and the woman in white fumbled with the release. When she was able to firmly grasp it, she yanked as hard as she could and toppled out of the car. She ran towards the only home she could remember knowing. Glancing back, she saw the man strumming his fingers on the steering wheel. He stared straight ahead, not even bothering to watch her. After several minutes, Jeffrey called out, "Ready or not, here I come." He floated free of the car and stood on his feet. Making a show of cracking his neck, though nothing cracked, he started for the abandoned house. Had he been a physical man with any sort of mass, his foot would have sunk through the rotting planks of the wraparound porch. Instead, he strolled across the deck and knocked on the door with a stern fist.

"Ms. woman in white, y'all home?" He bellowed with laughter, amusing himself. Jeffrey phased through the door and advanced into the living room. The place was ghastly and disgusting. It was in desperate need of torching. Bug infested furniture rested in the living room amidst the warped walls and peeling wallpaper. Rats nested in corners, bats clung to the ceiling, and mold covered almost every inch of the home. A fitting place for a ghost such as herself to haunt.

Jeffrey checked the kitchen first. He noticed a broken refrigerator with its door hung open like a gaping maw. A raccoon's nest rested inside. But he didn't much care for animals and nature. He had a blood lust that needed satiating, even in death. Stepping into the dining room, he grabbed a chair from under the rotting table and flung it hard against the wall. The soft wood splintered into wet, moldy chunks. A hole formed in the wall, letting in a small amount of moonlight. It shone where the chair used to sit.

"Are y'all under that table? I sincerely hope not. How cliché," Jeffrey said as he bent down to look. He smiled ear to ear when he saw the dark emptiness. "I am relieved to know y'all aren't that stupid." He moved on into the next room. The walls, floor, and furniture were so rotted, he couldn't tell what it was once used for. The woman in white couldn't be hiding here so he moved on.

The house had a cellar but Jeffrey decided to check upstairs first. He had a feeling about the cellar and knew she wouldn't hide down there. He guessed it was where her bones lay and ghosts tended to avoid their final place of rest. After all, that was the woman in white's story. Picked up by a hitchhiker and murdered in her own home. At least, that was *her* story. There were too many women in white for Jeffrey to count and he had slain several before her.

"I suppose y'all wonderin' why I'm doin' this?" Jeffrey said as he climbed the stairs. "I'd be lying if I was to say it weren't personal. But it is more than that. Death, well, she can't kill. Bound by some cosmic rule or somethin'. But lost souls, like y'all, upset the balance." He arrived at the top of the stairs and stood for a moment. "And Death loves her balance." With that, he continued down the hall.

A few rooms away from where Jeffrey now searched, the woman in white hid in a closet. She trembled uncontrollably. She didn't know ghosts could even tremble, let alone feel fear. But this man, this being, was worse than death. And if he got a hold of her, there was no telling what would happen. Was there another great beyond she would ascend to? Somehow, she knew the truth. There would be nothing after. There had been a chance to move on but she had ignored it. Her soul had nowhere left to go.

Her hands shook as she clasped them around her mouth. The man was in the room with her now, kicking bits of debris away. She begged and pleaded with whatever entity controlled the universe to spare her, to let her move on. She was sorry for the men she had killed after death. If there was a hell, her soul would go there. She could accept that. Hell was better than eternal darkness.

The man walked out of the room without checking the closet and her shaking subsided. If she had a heart, it would have been throbbing in her chest. Before she could relax, a pair of ghostly hands stretched through the wall from behind. They yanked her from the closet and into the next room. Standing over her was the man with the knife. She let out a wail that shook the foundation of the building. The man smiled and plunged the knife into her chest. She saw her body start to dissolve into mist and watched in horror as the man inhaled it all in.

"Keeps me in the astral plane," He said with a smile and the woman in white's world went eternally black.

Don't miss out!

Visit the website below and you can sign up to receive emails whenever Evan Bond publishes a new book. There's no charge and no obligation.

https://books2read.com/r/B-A-ZJVF-DVIXB

BOOKS 2 READ

Connecting independent readers to independent writers.

Did you love *Charred Remains*? Then you should read *Death Loves Her Balance*[1] by Evan Bond!

[2]

Read the short story that inspired the upcoming paranormal adventure by best selling horror author Evan Bond.On a dark stretch of road, a ghostly apparition appears to beckon lonely travelers. To the living, she is a lost hitchhiker in need of help. But she is something else entirely. Jeffrey stops to pick her up but there is more to him than meets the eye.

Read more at https://www.evanbondauthor.com/.

1. https://books2read.com/u/mgjwv6

2. https://books2read.com/u/mgjwv6

About the Author

Evan Bond is a thriller/suspense author who loves blending his love of the outdoors with his writings. He is the author of the best selling psychological thriller *Echoes of the Past* and his intense action-packed survival account *Death Can Wait.* He has always had a passion for telling suspenseful stories. Even at a young age, he was crafting horror stories to share with his family and friends. Evan Bond lives in Tampa, Florida with his wife, Melissa, their two boys, Desmond and Logan, and their cat and dog, Whiskey and Loki. When he's not writing, he can be found adventuring in the outdoors with his family and calling it "research" for his next novel.

Read more at https://www.evanbondauthor.com/.

www.ingramcontent.com/pod-product-compliance
Ingram Content Group UK Ltd.
Pitfield, Milton Keynes, MK11 3LW, UK
UKHW022024190726
13853UKWH00005B/2102

9 798330 367337